THE
LISTMAKER

· · · · · · · ·

Also by Robin Klein

People Might Hear You
Hating Alison Ashley
Halfway Across the Galaxy and Turn Left
Games . . .
Laurie Loved Me Best
Against the Odds
Came Back to Show You I Could Fly
Tearaways
All in the Blue Unclouded Weather
Dresses of Red and Gold
Turn Right for Zyrgon
Seeing Things
The Sky in Silver Lace

THE
LISTMAKER

. . . .

ROBIN KLEIN

VIKING

Viking
Penguin Books Australia Ltd
487 Maroondah Highway, PO Box 257
Ringwood, Victoria 3134, Australia
Penguin Books Ltd
Harmondsworth, Middlesex, England
Viking Penguin, A Division of Penguin Books USA Inc.
375 Hudson Street, New York, New York 10014, USA
Penguin Books Canada Limited
10 Alcorn Avenue, Toronto, Ontario, Canada M4V 3B2
Penguin Books (N.Z.) Ltd
Cnr Rosedale and Airborne Roads, Albany, New Zealand

First published by Penguin Books Australia, 1997
7 9 10 8 6
Copyright © Haytul Pty Ltd, 1997

Typeset in 12.5/16pt Goudy by Post Pre-press Group
Made and printed in Australia by Australian Print Group, Maryborough, Victoria

National Library of Australia
Cataloguing-in-Publication data:

Klein, Robin, 1936– .
The Listmaker.

ISBN 0 670 87175 3.

I. Title.

A823.2

For Brontye Cahill

1

. . . .

Moving-day checklist

At old address

1. Don't let Aunt Dorothy sit on any of the packed boxes in case of breakages.

2. Ring vet to make sure Horace isn't too upset about being left there. Remind him Horace won't eat any dried cat-food except kitten formula.

3. Pack separate box of afternoon-tea things for removalist people: instant coffee, teabags, biscuits, electric kettle, milk, sugar, teaspoons, cups, tea-towel – put in car boot. Also pack personal items needed while waiting at the new address for the van: something to read, fruit to eat (plus toothbrush and toothpaste for cleaning teeth afterwards), sweater in case of weather change, cleaning stuff (soap, sponge, broom, detergent, plastic gloves), tissues, memo pad and pen.

4. Drive to new address with aunts. Don't let Aunty Nat get out of the car even for *one minute*! She'll just skip around planning where to arrange the furniture. Send her right back *immediately* to previous address to finish off all the odd jobs there.

At new address

1. Sit Aunt Dorothy down somewhere out of the way. (NB Make sure she hasn't sneaked cigarettes in.)

2. Unpack box of afternoon-tea things. (NB Scrub down kitchen bench first.)

3. Check that water, gas, phone and electricity have been connected.

4. Ring vet to make sure Horace's condition hasn't changed since last call. (Remind him Horace might like a whisked egg for breakfast tomorrow morning as a change from kitten formula.)

· · · ·

There was no sign of Aunty Nat, even though it was an hour after the fixed time. She'd dropped us off at Avian Cottage so someone would be on hand for the furniture van when it arrived. 'Us' was me and her sister Dorothy. Aunt Dorothy was about as much use as a ladder without rungs, but I thought uneasily that it might have been better if they'd *both* gone back to the old address to make sure nothing was left behind. Then Aunty Nat wouldn't be on her own to deal with any emergency. Vacuuming, checking cupboards and saying goodbye to old neighbours shouldn't be taking her so long . . .

'I expect it's just some kind of trouble about fitting everything in the van,' Aunt Dosh said. 'No need for jitters yet, Sarah.'

'Who's jittery?' I demanded crossly. 'And there's no point unpacking the afternoon-tea things yet, not until that bench dries. I've just given it a good scrub with pine detergent. You can't be too careful about germs in a house that's been empty for months.'

I liked things to be tidy and hygienic. The most absolutely disgusting sight I ever saw was enlarged dust mites on a TV documentary. It upset me so much I bought a plastic mattress barrier, because Aunty Nat refused to give me one as a birthday present. She said that unless you were asthmatic, dust mites weren't anything to worry about. But then, *she'd* actually thought they looked kind of cute in that TV documentary – like herds of little grazing buffalo! Probably every surface in this old house was swarming with little grazing buffalo. I'd have to put up with them, too, for the whole of the summer holidays, because of staying with the aunts while Dad was overseas. He was often away on long business trips. Most term holidays and weekends I spent with the aunts, and the rest of the time I boarded at school, which I'd been doing ever since I was eight years old. For a couple of years before that, Aunty Nat had looked after me. There wasn't anyone else; my mother had died when I was five years old.

'Those biscuits are supposed to be for the removalists – if they ever get here,' I scolded Aunt Dorothy. 'If you're going to nick any, don't leave a trail of crumbs.'

You had to tidy up after her all the time. *Both* the aunts were exasperating in their own separate ways. Soon, though, things would be different. When Dad came back from this particular business trip he was getting married to Piriel Starr, and we'd all be moving to a city apartment. (Just us three, I mean. Not the ancient relatives – *they'd* be pottering around in this rackety old house Aunty Nat had bought.) Things would be different, and *wonderful*. I wouldn't have to board at school any more because it was fairly close to our apartment. I'd just be an ordinary student there from now on, coming home every afternoon. And I'd have the most glamorous new stepmother in the world, too. Piriel Starr – even her name was more distinctive than other people's! It was hard to believe that such exciting changes were about to happen in my life, and although I could hardly wait, I was also feeling a little bit nervous about the whole thing. It wasn't surprising, really. A set routine that had been going on for years was difficult to break, and deep down, I was secretly relieved to have a few more weeks with the aunts before my lifestyle changed.

'Eating sugar out of the jar!' I nagged. 'And you've gone and spilled some on the floor, Aunt Dosh.'

'I've got to do *something* if I'm not allowed to have a cigarette. Or even one lousy biscuit. They'll be tramping in with the furniture soon, so I don't know why you're fussing about a few little grains of sugar, Sarah. When I had my caravan, I only used to sweep it out once a week.'

Years ago, before moving in with Aunty Nat to keep her company, Aunt Dosh had been living in a tacky caravan park. At least Dad had said it was tacky. I didn't see it personally, because he'd never let me visit her there. (Come to think of it, neither had Dad.) He thought Avian Cottage wasn't much better than a caravan, either, and couldn't understand why they both wanted to move from Aunty Nat's comfortable brick unit. They'd been out on a drive, seen this old house for sale, and just decided on the spot that it was their dream home. Or at least Aunty Nat's ideal home – Aunt Dorothy floated around in a permanent dream of her own and didn't seem to mind where she lived.

I went out on the front porch to see if the furniture van was in sight yet. That porch looked like a battered old mantel clock. It had curly posts on each side with all the paint flaking off, and a name plate spelling out Avian Cottage in gold squiggles. (And in case you didn't know that 'avian' means birds, the metal door-knocker was shaped like a budgerigar to get the message across.) There was still no sign of the van,

5

though having Aunty Nat underfoot when you were trying to load up a pile of furniture might account for it being so late. Neither of the aunts were what you could call efficient.

Three examples (out of hundreds!):

1. Aunt Dorothy went into shops and couldn't remember what she'd wanted to buy in the first place.

2. Aunty Nat sometimes took her apron off and found another one underneath.

3. Once they'd gone to New Zealand for a holiday and it took them a couple of days to realise they had to adjust their watches.

But even for the most disorganised person, it was still only a half-hour drive at the most from the old address . . . I began to bite my nails.

Strangers were coming up the footpath. There was a man and a woman carrying an old swing-couch between them, and a kid about my age following behind with a stack of plastic cushions. They were talking to each other in that kind of shorthand people who belong together use, where you feel an outsider just by listening.

'Should have come back for the trailer.'

'Someone else might have got there first. Bit of a find, right on the holidays.'

'Can't it go in *my* room?'

'You've got enough junk in there already. The veranda, or maybe down under the ash tree. Get *off*, Corrie, you dag!'

'Carry me home the last bit. Go on, Dad, be a sport.'

'Let's park *her* out the front with a freebie sign.'

'No takers.'

'*Plenty* of takers. They'd think she was a garden gnome.'

Their hands touched as they put the load down and hoisted it up again. Their voices overlapped, blending into each other. You could tell they were a family, even without eavesdropping. The girl had one of those cheerful faces, all beams, big front teeth, and cheeks pushed up into shiny apples. I'd always found kids my age who looked like that a bit depressing. It was as though they were shining a torch right in my eyes. They hadn't noticed me on the front steps, and I was glad about it. If they were neighbours, I might have had to say hello, and I wasn't very good at stuff like that.

There was no sign of the van or Aunty Nat, so I occupied my mind by making a list. Lists were excellent therapy for any stressful situation. Like a visit to the dentist, for instance; an alphabetical list of clothing, multiplied by five, seemed to be just the right length for a dental check-up. By the time you'd got to

7

windcheater, waistcoat, waterproof coat, Wellington boots and wristband, the dentist had usually reached the stage of telling you to have a final rinse and spit. X, Y and Z were a bit of a challenge as far as clothing went; so were K, I and Q. But even after I'd managed to think up some new articles to meet that challenge, like X-ray gown, yashmak and zircon ring, Aunty Nat still hadn't come. I switched to an alphabetical careers list, sitting on the porch steps, where I could watch the road.

Admiral, baker, carpenter, dancer, engineer, factory worker . . .

Aunt Dorothy worked on a factory assembly line, putting electrical goods together. She'd been doing that same job for years, and never complained that it was boring. (Probably she liked it because microwave ovens and blenders didn't expect you to make conversation with them.)

Gardener, hairdresser, inventor, jackaroo, kindergarten teacher, laboratory technician, manager . . .

Dad was a section manager at the firm where he worked. I wasn't sure what he did exactly; it was something called marketing analysis. But I *did* know that to get promoted to section manager, you'd have to be highly organised and also punctual – not like Aunty Nat, who was an hour and a half overdue by now!

Naturopath, optometrist, police officer, real estate agent . . .

Piriel Starr was a real estate agent – and I bet she

would have made it all the way to being an admiral, too, if she'd ever thought about joining the navy instead. Perhaps I'd be a real estate agent/business executive like her when I left school, then I could have smart little cards with my name printed on them. When I'd mentioned that to Aunty Nat, though, she said twelve was far too young to be worrying about a profession, and that I should just 'light up' and enjoy myself more. (I think she really meant 'lighten up', but she often got trendy phrases wrong. I was pretty sure she wasn't referring to cigarettes, as she spent a lot of time trying to persuade Aunt Dorothy to give up smoking.)

'You've found a nice little possy, Sarah,' Aunt Dorothy said, clattering outside and sitting down beside me. 'You know, I think I'll go nuts if I don't have a cigarette!'

'You can't while you're wearing those nicotine patches. It said so on the packet.'

'The rotten things don't work like they claim they do.'

'Don't you *dare* peel it off! You've lasted since breakfast, so you can hang on a bit longer.'

'Maybe the chemist gave me a faulty batch . . .'

'They wouldn't sell people faulty ones, so don't make excuses. All you've got to do is think about something else. For instance, do you think twelve's too young to plan a career?'

'Can't say I ever thought about careers much when

I was your age. Homework was enough of a hassle to get through.'

'Piriel knew she wanted to be a businesswoman when she was still in primary school,' I said. 'She told me how it started. She auctioned off her Barbie doll collection and made over a hundred dollars. Charging extra for the ones with special features like Hawaiian suntan or crimped hair, of course. Then she put the hundred dollars in a high-return investment account. Don't you think that was smart for someone still in primary school?'

'She's a very smart cookie. I guess she's just one of those people who know how to get it all together,' Aunt Dorothy said, not sounding as impressed as she should have been.

Piriel was now one of the top sales people at an inner-suburban real estate firm which handled expensive townhouses, renovated warehouses and beautiful Edwardian mini-mansions. She knew just about everything there was to be known in the real estate business, just as she knew a lot about everything else, too. She could manage any situation with fingertip control.

The aunts didn't ever seem to be in control of situations – they just muddled through whatever was happening. Aunty Nat had even mucked up a simple little job like getting herself out of one house and into another! Maybe, though, something had gone seriously wrong and it wasn't her fault . . . Perhaps the removalists hadn't been sure of the way, so she'd volunteered to drive in front and show them. (Those removalists weren't even a proper professional firm out of the telephone directory, either. They were just a couple of unemployed nephews belonging to someone in Aunty Nat's card-playing group. She was doing them a good turn, so they'd have extra money for Christmas. The van was just a hired one, too.) There were a lot of steep roads in Parchment Hills, where Avian Cottage was. Maybe . . . maybe the van's brakes had failed coming down one of those hills and pancaked the little car the aunts shared between them to save on running costs. I suddenly saw objects littering a roadside, all in sharp detail, as though someone had just handed me a high-quality photograph. An embroidered spectacles case, a floral chiffon scarf, one shoe lying all by itself in the gravel, a handbag patterned with a big tyre mark . . .

'Stonemason, travel consultant, university professor, vet, weather forecaster, X-ray technician, yachtsman, zoologist,' I gabbled feverishly under my breath.

'If I'd had the choice of a career, I would have picked gardening,' Aunt Dorothy said. 'Oh look, there's a nice little clump of blue irises down there in all the weeds.'

She jumped off the porch to inspect them, and I went back inside to check that the phone was connected. Its last owner had decorated it with blue-wren stickers. They couldn't be peeled off, as I found after I'd dialled and waited a long time for someone to answer at the other place. No one did, which meant Aunty

Nat really *had* left. She just wasn't capable of ignoring a ringing telephone. She loved an opportunity to chat to anyone at all, even telephone sales people. (Dad claimed that he'd once overheard her earbashing someone who'd made an obscene phone call. Aunty Nat was kindly suggesting a whole lot of social clubs that creep could join, and also offering advice about where he could get counselling.) This time, though, the phone just rang and rang. If she'd already left, I thought anxiously, where was she *now*?

I hung up, debating whether to ring Piriel next. She'd given me one of her business cards, so I had her office, mobile phone and flat numbers. But I felt uncomfortable about bothering her. She might get the impression that her future stepdaughter wasn't capable of dealing with a small hiccup like a lost elderly relative and a missing truck full of furniture. Like Dad, Piriel had a low opinion of people who couldn't cope. The first time I met her was at a restaurant. Dad had arranged a special lunch to introduce us. When it was over, while he was paying the bill and Piriel and I were in the ladies' room, she'd smiled at me in the mirror and said, 'I don't particularly like children, Sarah; I might as well be frank about it. But you seem so sensible I just *know* we're going to get along very well indeed.' It felt like the highest kind of compliment, and I didn't want to risk damaging it now by sooking out my worries to her over the phone.

Actually, I'd already had plenty of training at being

sensible and self-reliant from four years of boarding school. Not that *everyone* who boarded there automatically developed those traits, of course; some of those girls were just as dizzy as the aunts! Because there was no one there I felt close to, I'd learned how to cope with day-to-day problems on my own. Just as I'd learned not to make a fuss about weekend treats being cancelled at the last minute because Dad had to work unexpectedly. He took it for granted I wouldn't complain about things. It was flattering, really, the way he treated me almost like another adult.

There certainly wouldn't be any hiccups when we moved into that city apartment – not with two capable people like Dad and Piriel in charge! There wouldn't be any snags at all during the actual move – or afterwards. Life would be as smooth as velvet in that apartment block with its high-tech security system, residents' pool and resident caretaker. That's what I felt like right now at Avian Cottage, a resident caretaker, though I wasn't making a good job of it. Clutching a germy telephone decorated with blue-wren stickers and worrying about a scatty old lady didn't seem very constructive. I took out the memo pad that went everywhere with me.

'Aunt Dosh,' I called through the front door. 'Let's make a list of everything in the house that needs repairs.'

It wasn't as though I thought she'd be much help with it, but I didn't want to risk leaving her outside by

13

herself. She was capable of wandering off to look at the other gardens in the street without telling me first. One missing aunt was quite enough to deal with.

'We'll start with this entrance hall,' I told her after I'd finished wiping up the soil she'd tracked back inside. 'You call out the things, and I'll write them down.'

'You and your lists! Well, all right, dear, but I'm not sure I can spot anything much. It all seems okay to me.'

'How about those cracks in the wall? And the light fitting . . .'

'Cobwebs can just be swept off.'

'I didn't mean cobwebs, I meant all those dangly glass teardrop things. Half of them are missing. And the floor dips down in one corner, surely you can see *that*?'

The floor sloped in the main bedroom, too. The wardrobe door was also stuck, though Aunt Dorothy claimed it just needed a good shove. When she tried, it came right off its track and crashed into the flywire screen on the window.

'Oops,' she said. 'Oh well, never mind. I think that screen needed replacing, anyhow. It was already full of holes, not just the one I made.'

I went through into the ensuite bathroom and tried the taps, which made a noise like a couple of Rottweilers. So did the overhead fan and the toilet when we tried flushing it. Someone had got a bit carried away using swans as a motif in that ensuite. They floated about on the tiles, shower curtain and blind, not to mention a plastic ornament clipped to the bath, shaped like a swan with its wings arched to hold soap.

Aunt Dorothy trailed after me back to the living room, which was painted pink, like the icing on little kids' birthday cakes. It had a narrow wallpaper strip pasted all around the walls, just under the ceiling. At first we thought the pattern was just roses or something. Aunt Dorothy hoisted herself up on a window ledge for a closer look, and said they were pink dancing flamingos. (She also managed to knock a curtain-rod loose when she was getting down.) *Anyone* could see that an urgent redecorating job was needed for the living room, so I didn't make any notes on my memo pad. I didn't bother making notes about the kitchen, either. It was just one big disaster zone. At least it didn't seem to have any birdy items anywhere – though the dining room opening off it certainly made up for that! It was lined with parrot wallpaper.

'Oh no, Sarah, we wouldn't want to rip down that nice wallpaper,' Aunt Dorothy objected, reading the list over my shoulder. 'It was one of the things that really caught Nat's eye when we were thinking about buying. She's going to make a matching tapestry cover for the window seat.'

There were more parrots, real ones, flitting about outside the big window. I watched them for a while, thinking they looked like little red jesters tumbling about amongst all the greenery. Avian Cottage was two-storeyed, but because it was built halfway down a slope, the top floor was the entrance with the other level tucked away underneath. The garden seemed to go on forever. It was actually a double block, the rear one just bushland. Being so high up, I was looking down into the tops of shrubs and even some of the trees. There were so many shades of green I could have used up a whole page of my memo book listing them all, but we still had to get the repair details for downstairs. (Piriel Starr, I knew, would never leave a job half-finished.)

The staircase leading downstairs had a banister knob missing, four wobbly steps, a broken light, and a loose shelf on the landing. That shelf was carved like an eagle with its wings spread wide, and could probably give people a nasty fright looming out of the shadows if the landing light wasn't fixed. (Aunt Dorothy went one better. She just about knocked herself out crashing into it.)

The bottom floor was where I gave up and put my pen away. Listing all the things wrong down there would have filled the whole notebook! Because of the wild green garden smothering every window pane, it felt like swimming about in a pool that hadn't been de-sludged for a long time. And as though there wasn't quite enough green outside, someone had even stuck up a rainforest scene in the end room. It was one of those enormous blown-up photograph posters, covering a whole wall. You could just about smell leaf-mould if you stared at it long enough – though maybe I was only imagining that because of the musty atmosphere downstairs. Aunt Dorothy did stare at it, going off into one of her trances because she thought it was so beautiful.

I went back upstairs, washed my hands thoroughly, then sat on the front porch again, thinking glumly that with Dad overseas, school closed for the holidays and Aunty Nat vanished from the face of the earth, I was more or less in the position of being an orphan. (Aunt Dorothy didn't count; no sane person would have given someone my age into her custody.) It was quite a battle to stop myself phoning Piriel and bleating about it. I was quite sure that if *she'd* found herself in a similar predicament at my age, she wouldn't have whinged about it to anyone. Somehow she would have known *exactly* what to do. So instead I made an irritated list of all the most annoying old-fashioned words and phrases still used by the ancient aunts, such as frock, wireless, rouge, all that glitters is not gold, stockings, every cloud has a silver lining. And by the time I'd reached all's well that ends well, a van came trundling up the hill followed by Aunty Nat's little car squeaking along behind like something out of Beatrix Potter.

2

. . . .

Irritating habits of elderly aunts

Aunty Nat

1. Getting slang expressions wrong and saying things like 'a real woozie' instead of 'a real doozie'.

2. Her real doozie of a cassette collection (played loudly in the car and when she's cooking): *The Three Tenors in Concert, Twenty-Five Favourite Hymns, Camelot, Aled Jones Boy Soprano, The Mikado, Magic Moments from Favourite Ballets, Phantom of the Opera, The Immortal Glenn Miller, Songs of the Scottish Highlands* etc.

3. Sending me down to video shops to get out nerdy videos: *Casablanca, Singin' in the Rain, The Great Caruso, Gone with the Wind, Ben Hur, The Greatest Story Ever Told, Seven Brides for Seven Brothers* etc.

4. Buying embarrassing things like treatment lotion for corns when I'm right next to her in a chemist shop.

Aunt Dorothy

1. Wearing old tracksuits instead of winter pyjamas.

2. Wearing checked flannel shirts and Blundstone boots.

3. Promising she's going to quit smoking on a certain date. Then when it arrives, saying her horoscope in the paper warns it's not such a good day to begin new projects.

4. Making *me* answer the door if it's someone selling stuff, because *she* never knows how to get rid of them.

• • • •

'All's well that ends well,' Aunty Nat said. 'Fancy those young idiots forgetting the patio furniture and having to turn around and go back for it!'

'If you'd taken Piriel's advice and hired a proper removalist firm . . .' I began sternly.

'Oh, I couldn't do that, Sarah, not after promising the work to Scott and Cameron. And they did a pretty good job on the whole, even if there *was* a spot of bother fitting everything in snugly. That was only inexperience, though, just little things like not taking the legs off the beds first. Still, we managed, and nothing much got damaged. It wasn't the boys' fault, either, the van conking out on such a narrow corner with me stuck behind. There wasn't a skerrick of room to overtake. We all just had to sit it out while Scott tracked down the engine problem. I was going to try reversing all the way down that bendy road and taking another route, but it was just far too dangerous with all the blind corners. I'm sorry you had such a long wait, dear, without any means of knowing what was going on. But there was no alternative.'

I thought of several (though Piriel explained to me once that the use of 'alternative' isn't strictly correct when there are more than two choices). It was a waste of time, however, pointing any of them out to Aunty Nat. She'd been having one dither after another ever since Scott and Cameron had unloaded all the stuff and taken themselves off. The present dither involved searching her handbag for the code list to find out which of the packed boxes held towels. I'd personally invented that code system of numbered stickers on all the boxes, and felt quite proud of it. Though it had clearly been a mistake to hand the important master list to Aunty Nat for safekeeping.

'The jolly thing's in here somewhere,' she said, upending her handbag over the kitchen table. It produced only recipes torn from hairdressing salon

magazines, brooches with missing pins that had probably been on their way for repairs months ago but
hadn't quite made it yet, bankcard slips, and a change-
of-address form which she'd forgotten to hand in at the
post office.

'Well, I guess I could dry myself on my shirt after
I've had a shower,' I said, being resourceful. (Piriel
Starr was resourceful at my age. She'd told me about
arriving once at a birthday party where another girl
was wearing an identical dress. So Piriel had ducked
into the bathroom and snipped away the top layer of
her own skirt with a pair of manicure scissors, leaving
just the lining. That had transformed it into a very
plain sheath dress, much more sophisticated than anyone else was wearing.)

'But I bought some new towels to celebrate our first
night in Avian Cottage,' Aunty Nat protested. 'You
deserve a nice one, love, after all your hard work showing Cam and Scotty where the furniture should go.
Let's see, perhaps they're in this carton marked *T2*.'

'I think that's your tapestries – or maybe tableware
stuff. If we only had that master list . . .'

'Quality towels they were, too; those ones that look
like velour. Watermelon-pink for my ensuite, moss-
green for you and Dorothy in the downstairs bathroom.
Because of all those darling little ferns peeping in at
the windows, you know.'

'They aren't little or darling, Aunty Nat. They're
huge great frondy things,' I said. 'And talking about

moss, I think it could be a bit damp downstairs. There's a funny smell.'

'Old houses are always on the nose after they've been closed up for any length of time. I'm sure it's only due to that. The agent said Avian Cottage is in fair enough condition if you take its age into account.'

I thought about producing my list of repairs, but it somehow seemed picky when she was so delighted at finally being in her dream house with everything unloaded, the van gone, and weeks of contented pottering to look forward to. She kept flitting about now to admire things she'd only just noticed, like a row of brass owl hooks behind the kitchen door. And for all I knew, the house *was* in good condition for its age.

The same thing, I suppose, could be said about Aunty Nat herself. She and Dorothy had been my mother's aunts, really, but Great-aunt was too much of a mouthful to say. For someone over sixty, she was very vain about her appearance, going to the hairdresser once a week. The hairdresser had invented this particular colour rinse for her, like rose-hip syrup. She wore rose-pink lipstick to match, mist-blue eyeshadow and floaty scarves. You had to give her credit for trying, although Piriel had remarked to me on one occasion that Aunty Nat really should do something about getting her weight down. Piriel claimed that all weight problems could be controlled by strict diet and a fitness program. I couldn't imagine *her* ever losing her figure, but Aunty Nat was as plump and round as Horace.

I'd been trying all day not to think about poor old Horace! You get very attached to a cat you've had for years, even if you see them only at weekends and in term holidays. Although he was officially mine, he'd always lived with the aunts because of Dad being away so often. (In fact Dad didn't like cats, and it was the aunts who'd actually given me Horace in the first place.) It had been their suggestion that Horace should stay overnight at the nearest vet's for this move, so he wouldn't get agitated by all the furniture being taken out of the only house he'd ever known. But I suspected he'd be just as agitated by having to spend a night at the vet's! Horace liked routine. He'd get upset even if his food bowl was moved to a different spot, or if a favourite cushion was at the wrong end of the couch. He *hated* change – though soon there'd be another one in his life, when I took him with me to live in the city apartment. He'd have to be trained to use a litter tray before then, too, and I wasn't sure how he'd take to that idea.

'It's certainly been a long day,' Aunty Nat said. 'I know it's not even dark yet, but having an early night seems like a good idea. Dorothy's mooning around outside somewhere, so maybe you could fetch her back in.'

Aunt Dorothy was hard to find in that big garden. Threading a way along the paths was like playing hopscotch. They kept disappearing under weed clumps and didn't keep in straight lines, but rambled about between shrubs and through overgrown archways that looked more like railway tunnels. There didn't even appear to be any proper flowerbeds, either. Plants just sprouted up out of the long grass, each one competing with the next, like sports teams. Only in this case the teams had all surged out of control and seemed to be bashing each other up. Two climbing roses along the side fence, one yellow and the other pink, had gone even further and reached the stage of strangling each other. I stopped to look at the roses, trying to work out if they were both on our property, or if the yellow one actually belonged to the house next-door. You would have thought that the people who'd originally planted them could have got together and chosen colours that didn't clash quite so much.

A big white cockatoo suddenly came flapping over the fence at me. I jumped, then blushed and pretended I'd only leaped aside to dodge rose thorns. It wasn't a cockatoo at all, just that beamy, bouncy girl I'd seen earlier. She was handing me scones wrapped up in a white tea-towel.

'Hi, I'm Corrie Ryder,' she trumpeted in the loudest, fastest voice I'd ever heard. 'Your next-door neighbour – well, I guess that's obvious, isn't it, otherwise I wouldn't be up on this fence! Mum says to yell out if there's anything you guys need. She would have brought these scones over herself, only Dad told her not to be a pest on the very first day you moved in. Rubbish collection's early Wednesday morning, mail gets delivered about ten, and if you like grapefruit, just help yourself off our tree. It sticks over your fence, anyway. Oh, and if you want to get rid of all those blackberries down the back of your place, I'll just bring Meg over some time. She *loves* guzzling them up. I'm twelve, by the way. How old are you?'

'The same,' I said guardedly. Having someone the same age as me next-door would almost certainly set Aunty Nat hinting that we should be friends. She was forever trying to push me into making friends with local kids, so I'd have someone to clack around with on weekends and holidays. (I think Aunty Nat meant 'hack' but she'd got the expression wrong.) Well, she needn't think this boomy-voiced Corrie Ryder was the answer to her prayers! I couldn't see us having anything at all in common. Corrie looked as though dust mites wouldn't bother her one bit. Even trying to make temporary friends with her seemed to be a wasted effort, because I wouldn't be here long enough. It might save time to make the situation clear right from the start . . .

'My name's Sarah Radcliffe,' I began. 'I saw you this afternoon carrying a couch thing along the street. It was while I was helping my aunts shift in, but I don't really live with —'

'Isn't it ace, that swing-couch? Some people round in the lane were chucking it out. Dad's already busted one of the chains swinging too hard, but he's going out to get another length. We're picking up our Christmas tree, too, at the same time . . . There he is now – gotta go, see ya!' Corrie babbled as a car horn tooted from around the front of their house.

She vanished down her side of the fence without giving me the chance to say anything at all. I was left staring up at the empty place where she'd been, thinking what patchy manners Parchment Hills people seemed to have. It wasn't polite to dart off like that in the middle of a conversation. It was even ruder to announce that you'd bring someone called Meg over to help herself to other people's blackberries without even waiting for an invitation! Perhaps, though, the Ryders didn't know any better. When he'd seen on the map how far Parchment Hills was from the city centre, Dad had made a joke about this area being full of wild hillbillies. He'd said that next time he caught up with them, the aunts would probably be wandering around barefoot with clay pipes wedged in their mouths.

Aunt Dorothy just about fitted in already with her nicotine addiction! Dad and Piriel didn't smoke, and neither did any of their friends; they wouldn't be seen doing anything so uncool. I could see a thread of smoke spiralling up from further down the garden. Aunt Dorothy, who didn't even seem to realise it was uncool, was sitting on a log just where the bush block began, lighting a cigarette from the stub of another. I hurtled down the rest of the path and made her put it out. There was never much point yelling messages at her from a distance. She always seemed to be enclosed in some kind of container, like those bottled sailing ships, and if you wanted to attract her attention, you had to get up close and sort of tap on the glass. It was hard to believe she was the sister of short, teapot-shaped Aunty Nat. Aunt Dorothy was tall and gawky and she hadn't been anywhere near a hairdressing salon for years. Her hair was just scraped back into a knot and shed hairpins like pine needles all day long.

'Moving day was the date we all picked for you to give up that disgraceful habit once and for all,' I said. 'What happened to the patch?'

'It's okay, I ripped the darn thing off first.'

'It's *not* okay. You're supposed to be a committed quitter now, with hours of clean air in your lungs.'

'I promise I'll try again tomorrow.'

'It's for your own good,' I said, nudging her back towards the house. It was like taking a brontosaurus for a walk. On the way there she managed to collide with a branch, a garden tap, an old wheelbarrow and the barbecue. A couple of bricks fell off the barbecue, but it didn't seem to matter very much. The whole thing was full of dead leaves from a huge tree that arched over the house like an extra green roof. The gutters were choked up with dead leaves, too, but instead of chopping that tree down, someone had stupidly built a seat all around its trunk. Aunty Nat, who'd come outside for one last gloat before going to bed, just said quaint little touches like that were what gave Avian Cottage its character.

'Here's another quaint little touch,' I said, handing

her the bundle of scones. 'Someone from next-door slung them over the fence at me, but you and Aunt Dosh are welcome to the lot. I don't want any, thanks very much. There's no way of telling how *clean* that tea-towel actually is.'

'Sarah, anyone would think germs have their own mafia with you as a personal target,' Aunty Nat said. 'This cloth is *perfectly* clean. It was very neighbourly of those people, and I hope you thanked them nicely. What with Dorothy being such a hermit and you acting so superior lately, it's a wonder we have any mates at all.'

'I do *not* act superior . . .' I began, but then stopped self-consciously, wondering if it was maybe true. Tara McCabe at school had called me a snob a couple of times. And once she'd snapped at me in the dining room, 'We're sick of hearing about your dad, Radcliffe! He's probably just as stuck-up and boring as you are!' At least that's what I *think* she said. Tara had shocking table manners and often talked with her mouth full. Perhaps she'd just been jealous that day because the mail had come and Dad had sent me a wonderful new watch, even though it wasn't my birthday or anything. Although Tara might have thought I'd been showing off, I was always more than willing to lend my things to her or anyone else. They could have even borrowed that new watch if they'd asked. (Dad must have forgotten he'd already sent me two duty-free watches on other trips he'd made overseas.) The only condition I ever set on people borrowing my things at school was that they should take good care of them, which I always explained very carefully beforehand.

But there wasn't much point defending myself to Aunty Nat right then. She'd spotted a sundial in a clump of daisies and gone dashing away for a closer look. After that it was a large shell someone had left under the garden tap, then a duck-shaped hose sprinkler. 'It's like hidden treasure!' she cried. 'Oh, isn't this thrilling – our very first night at Avian Cottage! Just for kicks, let's use one of the downstairs doors to get back inside!'

'Like astronauts hoisting a flag on the moon,' Aunt Dorothy said.

Dad often referred to the aunts as 'the girls'. Sometimes I thought it sounded a little bit patronising (even though I'm sure he didn't mean it to be), but it wasn't difficult to see why he called them that. I trailed through the fernery and out on to the back lawn after them, not because of wanting to join in any girlish games, but so their feelings wouldn't be hurt. That was one continuous job. For example, both of them had been terribly disappointed a few Christmas Eves ago when I'd told them they needn't bother making fake snowy boot prints for my benefit all around the house after I'd gone to bed. It was starting to get so *embarrassing*. Telling them I didn't believe in Santa Claus always seemed too brutal, so I'd have to pretend excitement about the boot prints next morning. Thank goodness they were finally cured of all that nonsense (though it had taken longer to stop Aunty Nat leaving a slice of Christmas cake and a glass of lemonade next to the fireplace).

Right now she'd just seen a metal rooster up on the roof. It was an ordinary weathervane, but because she hadn't noticed it before, you would have thought Santa Claus had called in a couple of weeks early and left it there as a present. Aunt Dorothy didn't burble on quite so much about this latest hidden treasure, but you could tell she loved Avian Cottage, too. Personally, I couldn't understand what they were so rapt about. Dad had already told me his private opinion – that buying a decrepit house with such a large garden was a ridiculous thing for someone Aunty Nat's age to do. He thought both the aunts should have had enough sense to move into a retirement village where they'd be properly looked after by qualified staff as they grew older. Piriel agreed with him wholeheartedly, adding that even though Aunt Dorothy hadn't actually stopped working yet, she should be making sensible plans for when it happened.

'Oh, we'll have such a football doing up Avian Cottage!' Aunty Nat said chirpily. 'All it needs is a lick of paint. And whatever colour we decide on, we could do that little lattice summerhouse to match. Goodness, won't it seem posh having a garden with one of *those*? The nearest we ever got to it before was a beach umbrella stuck up somewhere.'

The summerhouse, on a terrace halfway down the slope, really didn't look much different from a shabby old beach umbrella. Even though the light was fading rapidly now, the aunts showed signs of meandering down there through the knee-high grass for a closer inspection. I quickly pushed open the back door of the *real* house and shooed them in, suddenly scared by a vision of them vanishing for good in that dark wilderness, of not being able to find them. The door stayed open long enough for all of us to get inside, then lurched off one of its hinges.

'Oh well, I daresay we can fix that properly tomorrow,' Aunty Nat said, wedging it shut behind us with one of Aunt Dorothy's gardening boots.

'It's not the only door down here that needs fixing,' I said, taking her along to my room to show what I meant. That room had a stained-glass door, which was supposed to open into a little courtyard, but couldn't be budged. The frame seemed to have shrunk or something. (And I noticed, with a feeling of resignation, that the stained glass showed two magpies sitting on a branch.)

'Just needs a handyman with a plane,' Aunty Nat said. 'He'd better be careful not to break those nice leadlights, though. Maybe we could have panels made like that for *all* the doors, with different birds in each one. I must say, love, you've got this room looking shipshape. No one would believe you only moved into it this afternoon, everything so neat, all your clothes hung up so nicely.'

The room was the largest one downstairs, and I didn't feel comfortable about having it. It should have been Aunt Dorothy's, but she'd already chosen a little one tucked away under the staircase. She'd insisted that she was perfectly happy there, and had made me take the big end room with its enormous poster, built-in wardrobe and complete wall of shelves. It seemed mad. When I moved to the city this would just become a guest room, its spaciousness wasted.

'We'll get it all painted soon as Christmas is out of the way,' Aunty Nat said. 'Or you might like wallpaper instead, Sarah – though it would be a shame to get rid of that lovely forest picture. The final choice should be up to you, because it'll always be your room, dear. For when you come to stay with us on weekends and holidays, which I hope you'll still do. As often as possible.'

It wasn't likely. When I moved to the city I'd be far too busy to stay with the aunts very often. Specially at weekends. Piriel planned to do a lot of entertaining in that apartment; she'd said so. She'd need me around to help with that. And I'd be doing some entertaining of my own, because everyone at school would realise just how exciting my new lifestyle was. They'd be dropping hints for dinner invitations and to stay overnight. Things would be different then, because *I'd* be different. Somehow brighter and more interesting . . .

'Bare shelves never look quite right,' Aunty Nat said. 'You should unpack some of your books and knick-knacks.'

'It seems a waste of time when I'll have to pack them up all over again in a few weeks.'

'Well then, as soon as we find that code list thingummy, I'll give you my china animal collection for down here. It would be just perfect! Some of them even date back to when I was your age, though a few didn't survive having to share a room with Dosh then. I still remember what happened to my dear little Spanish donkey . . .'

'I didn't break that on purpose,' Aunt Dorothy defended herself. 'Anyway, it was a hedgehog.'

'It was a *donkey*, and I can remember as clear as daylight you knocking it off my bedside table.'

'Did not.'

'Pardon me for living, Dorothy Monaghan, but I can still see those broken pieces scattered all over the green lino! I remember picking up one poor little ear . . .'

'It was the red tiles in the kitchen, and it was a *hedgehog* – so there!'

I'd switched off. The aunts didn't exactly quarrel, but sometimes minor arguments would jump up out of nowhere, like bubbles in porridge. They never lasted very long, but were always so utterly juvenile it was best to pretend they weren't happening. I inspected the shelves, even though it seemed about as pointless as taking an interest in some motel room. Still, I thought, I might as well put out one or two of my own things (after I'd given each shelf a good scrub down, of course). Certainly not Aunty Nat's china animal collection, which was *gross*.

'Oh, come and look, Dosho! You never saw such a beautiful moon!' Aunty Nat cried, and they both crowded to the window. They stood there close together, exclaiming softly, as though they hadn't even been bickering just two seconds ago.

'Millions of stars, too,' Aunt Dorothy said. 'They seem to sparkle more up here, because the air's so clear. I'll trim the ferns away a bit tomorrow, then Sarah will be able to fall asleep watching the stars.'

'That's if I don't fall out of bed first,' I said. 'In case you haven't noticed, the floor's so slanty in here it looks like something out of Luna Park.'

'There certainly does seem to be a little problem with the floors not being level,' Aunty Nat said. 'We won't worry about it tonight, though. Shove something under the bed legs at the other end, dear, so it's more on an even keel. The estate agent said it's only some of the stumps under the house need replacing, and I've already booked someone to come and have a squiz tomorrow. I think you call them re-blockers. He's not just a re-blocker, though; he does all sorts of other odd jobs, too.'

'There's probably enough of those to keep him busy here for weeks,' I said, yawning. 'He'll still be here even after I'm gone, most likely, so I'd better give you this list I made of all the repairs. It's not as though I'll be around to –'

'I'll just check if the water's hot enough for your shower, Sarah,' Aunty Nat interrupted and bustled out as though it was the most vitally important thing in the world. Aunt Dorothy went, too, but first she did an odd thing for her. She frowned at me over her shoulder.

'What's that for?' I asked, surprised.

'For being so dense about certain things,' she said reprovingly. 'People's feelings, I mean.'

3

· · · · · · · ·

Boarding at school

Minuses

−1. Not having Horace there.

−2. When they're all giggling and won't tell me what the joke is. Or – when they're all giggling and I *know* what the joke is (eg Tara McCabe pretending to be me trying to play tennis).

−3. Tara claiming I was blubbing after lights out. I was *not*. It was only hay fever. It wasn't anything to do with the ski weekend. (Tara should just mind her own business and stick to horses!)

−4. The way Mrs H. seems to look down her nose a bit when the aunts come to collect me. The way Mrs H. *doesn't* look down her nose when it's Dad picking me up in the company car.

−5. Hearing day-kids say they're going shopping or something with their mum after school.

Pluses

+1. It's a weight off Dad's mind when he has to go away so much.

+2. He doesn't think it would work out if I lived *all* the time with two old ladies.

+3. Mrs H. is usually very nice. It's only every now and then she acts snobby and has favourites.

+4. The day-girls all think it must be so terrific living in the boarding house.

+5. It's all over now, anyway – starting from next term! (So I don't even know why I'm bothering to make this dumb list!)

· · · ·

Well, I should have realised that any vet in a backward suburb like Parchment Hills wouldn't be efficient! They'd just ignored what I'd said about Horace needing a room all to himself. When I went to collect him, I found they'd kept him there overnight next to a Siamese kitten! Although they were both in separate wire cages, poor Horace looked scared out of his wits.

(Kittens, guinea-pigs and goldfish had that effect on him; so did people pulling tissues out of boxes.) He made a pathetic hostage kind of noise when he saw me, and I felt the vet should deduct something off the bill for being so slack. I didn't have quite enough nerve to say so at the desk, and the receptionist didn't give me a chance, either. She was up on a chair prising drawing pins out of a wall poster. It was a chart of native birds, which she handed to me rolled up in an elastic band.

'Your aunt asked if she could have it yesterday,' she explained. 'While you were in the other room all that time saying goodbye to your cat. I would have got it down for her then, but the phone kept ringing. It's a bit worse for wear, but she's welcome to it.'

I handed over the cheque for Horace, feeling embarrassed. The waiting room was full of people, just as it had been yesterday. I certainly couldn't imagine Piriel Starr doing such a thing, asking if she could have a tatty old poster to keep! It was awkward to carry, too, because I needed both hands for the pet basket. Horace wasn't the slimmest cat in the world. Aunt Dosh had offered to collect him by car, but I knew from experience that walking home was better. Horace tended to be neurotic in the car after a vet visit. He seemed to think you'd drive around in a circle and take him straight back there. Not that he was much calmer being lugged along in his basket, but at least he didn't thrash around quite so much.

I kept stopping every now and then to pat him, so

he'd save his nervous breakdown for some other time. The basket was getting heavy. Halfway along, I had a rest on a bench outside the post office. Horace peered out through the wicker slats at the Parchment Hills residents trickling lazily past, and it seemed to settle him down. Maybe it was the slow-motion way they walked. No one seemed to be in any hurry – perhaps because there wasn't anything interesting enough in the area to hurry *to*. Parchment Hills was even further away from the city than the aunts' last address. I knew they couldn't really afford to move closer in, but their last place being so inaccessible had been one of the reasons why I boarded at school. Living there would have meant hours of daily travel. That didn't stop Aunty Nat, though. She kept nagging Dad to let me move to a school nearer to where they lived, but he'd always change the subject. I hated them arguing about it.

Anyway, it seemed silly to upset a perfectly good arrangement that was working okay, so I didn't raise any objections about boarding at school. Aunty Nat worried about it far more than Dad ever did; whether I was happy, if they looked after us when we felt ill, if I was getting enough to eat. (One good thing about being a day-girl next term would be no more of her wanting to know every little detail of school meals!) Next term, however, wouldn't happen for a long time yet; there were all the summer holidays to be got through first. I took out my pocket-sized organising planner, which I'd been inspired to buy when I first met Piriel. She had a fabulous digital one with her name and business address engraved on the front.

'Hi, Sarah . . . That's some cat you've got there! What's its name?'

'Horace, and he doesn't like strangers patting him,' I warned, but Corrie Ryder, having slammed noisily out of the post office, was already scratching Horace behind one ear. Surprisingly, he didn't seem to mind all that much. He just blinked at her with his big golden eyes.

'How come you're lugging him around in a carry basket? He looks like that wimpy lion in *The Wizard of Oz*.'

I glanced at her suspiciously, inclined to be defensive where Horace was concerned. Usually people tended to grin when they first saw him. There was no denying he was a bit strange with his orange fur, dinner-plate paws, and huge white ruff like a choirboy. Aunty Nat always claimed he looked like a stuffed toy for keeping pyjamas in. Corrie didn't sound as though she'd meant an insult, though, and was scratching him behind the other ear now.

'I've just picked him up from the vet. He stayed there overnight so he wouldn't get upset about moving,' I said, leafing through my organising planner, which wasn't in the same class as Piriel's. Mine was just a plastic wallet/notebook affair, but it had a telephone section, a three-year appointments diary, an international telecommunications guide, a row of key clips and a combination biro/pencil that fitted into a slot down one side. Boarding school wasn't exactly a social whirl, so most of the appointment pages for the last few months were blank. The only entries were for weekends spent with the aunts, Belinda Gibbs's birthday party, and a weekend when Dad said I could go skiing with him and Piriel. I'd outlined that date with asterisks.

It hadn't actually happened, though, because Piriel rang to say there'd been a complication. She'd forgotten to tell Dad that the chalet where she'd made reservations had an adults-only booking clause. To make up for any disappointment, she promised the three of us would have a whole week away together next snow season. It *was* disappointing, because I'd really been looking forward to it and had already started packing. Tara McCabe, my room-mate at the boarding house, offered to lend me her quilted jacket. Unfortunately, she got very annoyed when I washed it under the shower in readiness, although that jacket certainly needed a good scrub. Tara used it for riding in the holidays. She'd brought it to school with her so she could sleep with it under her pillow and think about her pony back on her parents' farm. (The whiff, actually, was like a whole *herd* of horses!) She snatched the jacket back, then flounced off and told everyone I'd just about come right out and said she *ponged*. After a couple of days I found ways of dealing with the disappointment. Going skiing next winter would probably be better in the long run, anyway. It didn't matter that no one else was likely to lend me their jacket after what Tara said; next snow season I'd be living in the apartment, and Piriel would help me shop for one of my own. It would also mean more time to get over feeling nervous about the idea of skiing and perhaps making a fool of myself in front of Piriel. (*She'd* done competition skiing when she was still in her teens, but if other sports were any clue, I wasn't sure *I'd* be much good at it.)

It was kind of depressing staring down at those blank appointment pages. There weren't many entries in the telephone section, either; just Dad's local, interstate and overseas contact numbers, a couple of girls from school, my dentist, and the aunts' phone number from their last place. I rubbed that out and pencilled in the new one for Avian Cottage. Piriel had advised using pencil. People, she said, tended to be mobile these days, not living in the one place for very long, and if you didn't have an electronic planner like hers, biro could look messy for information that might not be permanent. Even so, I hadn't used pencil to jot down *her* number; I'd entered it in my neatest writing with a calligraphy pen. (I'd also borrowed that calligraphy pen from Tara McCabe, and she'd said quite snakily when handing it over, 'Maybe you'd prefer to disinfect it first.')

'Are you checking who you have to send Christmas cards to?' Corrie asked. 'I've just posted mine off, though they're kind of weird this year. I made them out of noodles pasted on cardboard.'

They certainly did sound peculiar, I thought, getting up. Corrie Ryder was a bit weird herself, the way she'd plonked herself down and started chattering when we didn't even know each other or anything. Asking this and that, peering into private memo books . . .

'It wasn't for Christmas cards, just checking a telephone number. I'm just about to give my stepmother a ring. So I might as well use the post-office phone, seeing it's handy,' I said, as a hint that she could take herself off now.

'A stepmother? I didn't know you had –'

'Well, Piriel's not exactly my stepmother yet, but the wedding's early February. She's more like a best friend, really. We're going to be doing heaps of things together over the holidays. Maybe even this weekend.'

'Jeez, how did she make it through school with a name like *that*! I always reckon mine's funny, but *Piriel* . . .'

'Piriel happens to *like* her name – and so do I.'

'Well, whatever she's called, I'll mind Horace on the bench if you want to ring her.'

I hesitated, but felt I had to go into the phone box now I'd mentioned it. Phoning Piriel on a Saturday was out of the question, though. It was her busiest day of the week for showing properties to buyers. I'd actually watched her in action once, in between going out for

44

lunch with Dad and being dropped off at the aunts'.
(The original plan was that as it was a long weekend, I
could stay at Dad's flat. That had fallen through because
he had to work on an important report, so the lunch was
a kind of consolation outing.) On the way to the aunts',
we'd called in to see Piriel at this cool townhouse open
for inspection. That day she was wearing a linen suit
with a shirt the same deep, rich shade of burgundy as her
hair. Her only jewellery was a long gold chain and the
engagement ring Dad had given her. Somehow it looked
exactly right, and I'd felt choked with pride knowing
she'd soon be part of our family. She was far too busy to
chat when we dropped in, though she and Dad held
hands for a few minutes behind her beautiful slim-line
briefcase, which was reassuring.

Sometimes I needed little signs like that to con-
vince myself the wedding really *was* going to happen.
It all seemed too wonderful to be true – Dad getting
married again and all of us settling down in a permanent home. Next year, because I'd change into a
completely different person from Piriel's influence, my
wallet/planner would always be chock-full of appointments and telephone numbers.

Inside the booth, I glanced back at Corrie. Horace
had fallen asleep, either hypnotised from watching the
snail pace of Parchment Hills or because he liked having
his ear scratched like that. It seemed a good chance to
ring some of the girls from school and give them my temporary holiday number. Phoning from Avian Cottage

didn't seem advisable. Aunty Nat would be sure to suggest inviting them out to visit, and I didn't want anyone from school knowing I had relations who lived in such a shabby old house. It wasn't altogether snobbery on my part, either. That school was kind of posh. Some kids tended to stare a bit at the aunts when they dropped me off there. Not in a really rude way, but you could tell they thought the aunts didn't somehow quite fit in. Avian Cottage *was* a dump, but I didn't want the aunts' feelings hurt by outsiders maybe saying it out aloud. There certainly wouldn't be any danger of them thinking that about the city apartment, but in the meantime, all I wanted was someone to go to a movie with occasionally.

First I rang a day-girl called Marnie Kydd. Her mother answered the phone, and had to go off to hunt for her. She came back sounding flustered. 'I'm sorry, dear,' she said. 'I could have *sworn* Marnie was in her room, but now she seems to have vanished into thin air!' It had really been a waste of time calling in the first place, I thought. Just about every other occasion I'd rung before, nobody seemed to know where Marnie had got to!

I called Belinda Gibbs next. One of her little brothers answered and said, 'Yeah, what ya want?'

'This is Sarah Radcliffe. May I speak to Belinda, please?' I asked politely, trying to keep in mind that small children learn by good examples being set. (Not that Timothy Gibbs would find many set at his house, as I'd noticed when I went to Belinda's birthday party.

It was an expensive-looking modern house with a tennis court out the back, but I'd actually been quite pleased when that headachy party finished and I could go back to the orderliness of boarding school.)

'Hang on a bit,' Timothy mumbled, sounding as though he could have been gnawing on a slice of pizza and dribbling bits of it into the phone. He was gone for a long time. I began to think he might have been sidetracked and forgotten all about me. Their household was pretty casual, with everyone obviously allowed to do anything they wanted. Some kind of noisy background argument was going on there now, but eventually Timothy picked up the phone again and said, 'She's busy putting a bandage on our dog – he just got skittled by the motor mower.'

'Oh,' I said. 'The poor little thing . . .'

'No worries – what's a bit of blood and guts? See ya.'

I hung up, feeling puzzled, because I'd *distinctly* heard their dog barking in the background. It sounded an ordinary, cheerful kind of bark – not the kind a dog would make after being run over by a motor mower. Still, everything was so rackety at their house you probably couldn't count on normal reactions from the family pets.

I also had Tara McCabe's number, but there didn't seem much use ringing her. She lived on a sheep property in Gippsland somewhere. (Besides, even before the jacket incident, she kept dropping hints that she might move into the big dormitory next term, with

Lauren Gray and all that horsy lot. So next term she mightn't even want to know me.) Seeing there was no one else to call, I left the phone box.

'That phone's dodgy sometimes, it cuts you off right in the middle,' Corrie said. 'Did you get through to your stepmother?'

'Yes, no worries. She's picking me up late tomorrow afternoon. We'll probably go out for dinner some-where, then to a show,' I said, then stopped, wondering why I'd come out with all that. It wasn't as though it was any of Corrie Ryder's business.

'Oh, that's too bad. Some kids from my school are coming round tomorrow for a video night. You could have come over, too.'

I had to pretend what a pity it was all the way back to Avian Cottage. Corrie had finished her messages, so she was going home at the same time, and although it was easier carting Horace up that long hill with some-one else sharing the load, I felt edgy. Aunty Nat might just happen to be looking out the kitchen window. If she saw me strolling along with a local kid, she'd prob-ably rush out and invite Corrie inside for morning tea, lunch, the rest of the afternoon and maybe to stay the night as well. But luckily, she was nowhere in sight. I dumped Corrie firmly at her front gate, turning down her offer to help carry Horace the rest of the way and get him settled in.

There was a utility truck parked in our drive, which meant that the re-blocker must have arrived. Someone was tapping away at things under the house, with Aunty Nat's muffled voice supplying a running commentary. (I hoped she hadn't been optimistic enough to try and squeeze through the little access door.) I would have liked to go around the back to make sure she'd remembered Piriel's advice, which was that people should always get at least three quotes for any repair work, otherwise they could be ripped off. But Horace was more important.

I took him inside and downstairs, where I'd already set up his water bowl, sleeping basket and a litter tray. Cats, I knew, should be kept inside any strange house for a couple of days until they got their bearings. With Horace, I suspected that might take a whole lot longer, because much as I loved him, there was no denying he was a bit dim as far as cats went. He certainly showed no interest in getting orientated straight off. I couldn't even prise him out of the carrier until Aunt Dorothy came in through the back door to retrieve a cigarette hidden in the soap dish (even though she'd sworn faithfully last night she'd flushed them all down the toilet). Back doors don't normally open directly into bathrooms, but Avian Cottage followed its own strange rules. She fielded Horace's panicky dash for freedom and held him gently against her shoulder. He stopped twitching his tail and began to purr. For a person who couldn't walk down a supermarket aisle without knocking tins off shelves, Aunt Dorothy didn't show any clumsiness at all with animals.

'That re-blocking man's here,' she whispered. 'Mr Woodley, his name is. It was *awful*, Sarah – I had to talk to him all by myself until Nat finished having her shower!'

I'd made a list for her once, suggesting remedies for shyness. Some of them were excellent ideas, like joining a public-speaking group, but she hadn't really tried very hard so far. Her idea of a social life was a pre-breakfast swim, because hardly anyone else went to council pools so early. If we went out anywhere together and had to ask for directions, she'd make *me* do it. Even when we'd all celebrated Dad and Piriel's engagement at a restaurant in town, she'd blushed every time Piriel tried to include her in the conversation. It wasn't because Piriel was alarming or anything; Aunt Dorothy was so shy she didn't like speaking to strangers over the phone, either. Usually she wouldn't even answer it if Aunty Nat was out. So I could see that having to deal with an unknown tradesman must have been as much an ordeal for her as poor old Horace's stay at the vet's (but it still seemed ridiculous for someone her age).

'He kept calling out things from under the house,' she added. 'And I didn't know if he was just talking to himself or expecting me to make comments back. Am I glad Nat's taken over! She *always* knows what to say to people, so now I can get on with my gardening in peace.'

I followed her outside to have a look for myself, first

making sure the bathroom door was as tightly shut as it could be with only one hinge. Aunt Dorothy scuttled off down to the terrace, but I joined Aunty Nat at the access door. She looked bewildered, and it wasn't hard to understand why. Mr Woodley, crawling about under the house with a torch, seemed to be yelling at her in a foreign language.

'One bearer's a dead-set goner and the joists don't look too crash hot, either,' he shouted. 'Not to mention that slab work further along – the airhead who laid that oughta be pilloried!'

'What on earth is he talking about, Sarah?' Aunty Nat whispered.

I scrambled under the house to find out. Mr Woodley might be thinking that all his Christmases had come at once with only two vague old ladies to deal with. The sooner he realised they had someone capable of looking after their interests, the better for him! He was scraping the soil away from a post, which looked quite ordinary above the ground, but was worn into a spindle shape underneath.

'Is that the stump that has to be fixed? They'll be pleased you found it so quickly,' I said, holding my nose. (The ground below Avian Cottage was really more like a big pond of stagnant water.)

'*One?* The whole blooming lot have to come out,' Mr Woodley said rather crushingly.

He began to prod with a screwdriver at a long beam thing just overhead, showering us with little damp black flecks. I crawled back out hastily, and he followed, but didn't stay put. He set off around the outside of the house, kicking at bits of it every now and then. Then he wandered about on the back lawn, probing it with a long metal stick. Aunty Nat trailed after him uncertainly, and so did I, feeling quite protective. Mr Woodley *looked* honest enough. He would have made a very convincing department-store Santa Claus if you put a white beard on him. But if he had any secret plans for overcharging, he'd find it a lot harder with someone whose stepmother-to-be was a real estate executive staring him straight in the eye. He went down the steps to the terrace and aimed a kick at its retaining wall. Aunt Dorothy, who was snipping away at some vines there, dropped the secateurs from nervousness.

'Er . . . about the house,' Aunty Nat said, no longer able to bear the suspense. 'Were you able to find out what's making the floors slope, Mr Woodley?'

'Just call me Ed,' Mr Woodley said. 'And first things first – did I happen to hear someone mention a cup of tea?'

4

. . . .

Useful proverbs

1. Perseverance is the bridge by which difficulty is overcome.

2. Never put off till tomorrow what you can do today.

3. A great ship needs deep waters.

4. Who never tries cannot win the prize.

5. If at first you don't succeed, try, try again.

Action stations

1. Solve nail-biting habit! (Gloves in bed, soap under fingernails, willpower, 20 cent fines.)

2. Stop taking teddy bear to bed. (Childish.)

3. Find a library book about wine (to know what Dad

and Piriel are talking about in restaurants).

4. Start a get-fit, stay-thin exercise program. (Don't eat so many of Aunty Nat's donuts, either!)

5. Stop checking up in the middle of the night that the aunts haven't died in their sleep from old age.

• • • •

'This living room looks like a bunker lined with sandbags. I bet Piriel wouldn't dream of inviting visitors before everything's been unpacked.'

'Piriel won't even *be* here,' Aunty Nat said huffily. 'She hasn't got anything to do with my card nights, either. And if you're suggesting I cancel just because of a few stray boxes, Sarah, I'll have you know my monthly card nights are a *tradition*. There's been the odd occasion when someone couldn't turn up, like poor Derek with his hip replacement last year, but they're very rare. Those boxes won't upset anyone. Supper's always the main thing, anyway.'

She'd spent all afternoon baking. Aunt Dorothy hadn't helped with that; she was hopeless at cooking unless it was sausages, chips and frozen peas. Aunty Nat's cooking was altogether different. The dining-room table was spread with one of her embroidered cloths, edged so thickly with crochet lace that it looked like a coastline at high tide. The tide had cast up cucumber sandwiches, savoury rolls, meringue shells

54

filled with hazelnut cream, chocolate orange truffles, brandy snaps, and a sponge cake as big as a tricycle wheel.

'Our first card night in Avian Cottage deserves a good spread,' Aunty Nat said rather smugly. 'But goodness, just look at the time, and here's me with no warpaint on yet – let alone my girdle! Duck downstairs and make sure Dosh has changed into something halfway respectable, will you, love? I *did* remind her earlier, but you know what she's like.'

I had to wriggle past the two card tables to reach the staircase. They were wedged together to make one large cosy one, loaded with pencils, score papers, bowls of nibbles, drink coasters and Aunty Nat's gambling money. (She kept it in a plastic container she got from playing the poker machines somewhere, and it made the room look disgracefully like a casino.)

Bird motifs flitted about all over the place. She'd bought some new penguin-shaped drink coasters, plus a wooden card box with a mother-of-pearl peacock on the lid. Piriel's taste certainly didn't include objects like that. I'd been with her once while she bought a house-warming gift for someone where she worked. She'd chosen a set of very plain, straight-sided water glasses made from thick glass. Everything in that shop had been plain and beautiful: wooden bowls, white china, cutlery as simple as feathers. (Aunty Nat's teaspoon handles were all decorated with little wildflower badges – though most likely she'd be hunting around for ones with kookaburras on them now!) But it didn't really matter, I reminded myself. Soon I'd be living somewhere else, where tables would be set with flair and style . . .

I went downstairs to hurry Aunt Dorothy along, and it was just as well I did, because she hadn't even changed yet. She was just sitting on her bed reading a gardening magazine, with Horace curled up next to her. (Shutting him in the bathroom hadn't really worked. He kept getting stuck under the bath, so we'd had to give him the run of the rest of the house.)

'Dutch box has a pretty leaf,' Aunt Dorothy said. 'But then lavender would make a nice low hedge, too. What do you think, Sarah?'

'What I think is that they're all going to stare if you go upstairs and play cards in that holey old slip,' I said. 'It's nearly quarter to eight, you know. *And* you've been smoking in here again! Spraying insect repellent around isn't going to fool *anyone*.'

She put the magazine aside reluctantly and just grabbed the first thing in her wardrobe.

'Not that skirt, Aunt Dosh. The hem's come down.'

'Oh rats, so it has. But no one's likely to notice sitting round the card table, are they?'

'They'll notice the top half of you, so you can't wear that shirt, either. Two of the buttons are off.'

Aunt Dorothy stood there looking helpless, like a toddler having to be got ready for playgroup. I began at one end of the wardrobe and worked systematically

56

along the hangers, but as there weren't many, it didn't take long. Most of her clothes seemed to have creases, zippers that didn't work or pockets dangling from a few loose threads. But halfway along, crammed underneath a terrible old duffle coat no one could coax her to throw out, there was a fairly decent dress which Aunty Nat had made for her last summer. It hadn't been worn yet, and looked rather nice when she put it on. I even managed to find the belt that went with it, stuffed into the toe of a shoe.

'Do I have to wear one of those?' she grumbled. 'They always dig into your bellybutton when you sit down.'

'It's *meant* to have a belt – that's what those little loops on the waist are for, in case you haven't realised,' I said firmly, drawing it into the last notch. 'There, that's not too bad at all. You should wear blue more often, Aunt Dosh. It kind of suits you.'

'I never even know what it means about colours suiting people, though your dad's new girlfriend's always going on about it, too. I'm going to have to take your word for it, anyhow, with the light in here being so crook.'

'Maybe it can be moved to a different spot, not stuck away behind that rafter.'

'The whole wiring should be checked, really. I suppose Mr Woodley might know a good electrician. He's coming along tonight, as a matter of fact; Nat invited him on the spur of the moment. When he was here giving the quote, she found out he likes playing cards.'

I seemed to remember Dad telling Aunty Nat once that it wasn't a good idea to mix business relationships with social ones. (But it was a waste of time; she even used to invite the postman in for morning tea at their last address.) Aunt Dorothy's hair was a mess. She obviously intended to blunder upstairs with no more attention given to it than a few extra hairpins, but I made her sit down while I did it properly. Her hair was quite nice for someone her age, and it was a pity she didn't look after it better. It had a silvery/blonde/brownish sheen like new mushrooms. I made a French braid, feeling proud of myself for knowing how to do it from watching Piriel, who sometimes wore her hair that way. Piriel kept her hair shoulder length. She said it was versatile for choosing different styles to suit every possible social occasion. Some day I planned to get my own hair cut shoulder length, too. At the moment, all that could be said about it was that it was just long, clean, straight and neat.

'Now you've made me look like something out of *The Sound of Music*!' Aunt Dorothy complained ungratefully, but I pushed her upstairs before she could undo any pins. Cars scrunched the driveway gravel, which meant the visitors were starting to arrive. Aunty Nat would most certainly take them on a conducted tour all over her dream house, and I didn't think I could stand another dose of her raving on about the pelican wall tiles which had recently been discovered in the downstairs bathroom. (They were hidden behind an old airing cupboard which Aunt Dorothy careered into and knocked off its moorings.) Going upstairs later and saying a polite hello to everyone would be quite enough to put up with, so I slipped out into the moonlit courtyard and hid behind one of the ferns.

The courtyard was looking much tidier. I thought it was a crazy way for anyone to spend the first week of their annual holidays, but Aunt Dorothy seemed to enjoy it. She'd trimmed the branches crowding the window, and begun weeding. You could see the original paving stones now, and a little round flowerbed in the centre. She'd suggested I might like to choose some plants to go in that round bed, because the courtyard was *my* part of the garden. It really wasn't, because I wouldn't even be living at Avian Cottage in a few weeks' time. One of us would have to do something about putting in some plants soon, though, I thought critically; empty flowerbeds looked just as forlorn as bare shelves. I had plenty of time to gaze at it, because Aunty Nat didn't exactly hurry through her conducted tour. The room-to-room progress could be mapped by the visitors' squawks of admiration (they all had much the same taste as Aunty Nat), and when they'd all squawked through the downstairs part and then returned to the living room, I sneaked back inside.

I'd made a list of jobs to fill up my evening while they played cards. The first one was sorting out my school things ready for next term. That usually would have meant covering work files and books with new adhesive paper, but next term we'd all be using notebook computers instead, hired through the school. They were taking a big risk, I thought, trusting such expensive equipment to people like Belinda Gibbs, who never even looked after her *own* belongings. I was always careful with mine. Every weekend, I'd empty my schoolbag, brush it out, sharpen every pencil, test each biro to make sure it still worked, then throw out the ones that didn't, plus any scraps of loose paper. (I was always telling Aunty Nat she should do the same with her handbag, but she never got around to it.) This evening seemed a good opportunity to give my schoolbag an extra thorough cleaning, so I scrubbed it inside and out with pine detergent, then left it drying in the bathroom.

The next job was checking through a carton full of personal items, to make sure they'd come through the move undamaged. (We'd finally found the master code list. Aunty Nat had slipped it inside the food processor so it wouldn't get lost. Then, of course, she'd packed the food processor in an unmarked box.) None of my things were broken, because I'd wrapped them individually in tissue paper and also plastic bubble wrap. (A job worth doing is worth doing well.) I meant to repack them straight back into the carton ready for the apartment, but then glanced up at the wall of empty shelves. It wouldn't be too inconvenient to leave at least *one* thing out on display. I chose a framed photo of Horace taken when he was a kitten. Aunty Nat had given me the frame, shaped like a cottage window with a pot of geraniums in one corner. Aunt Dosh had taken the photograph, which explained why it was a bit out of focus.

Then I set out clothes for tomorrow, copying Piriel, who always did that after watching the weather forecast. She said it saved time. She'd also told me that an enormous collection of clothes wasn't necessary for *anyone*. (Though I knew she didn't mean to take Aunt Dorothy as an example and get by with a few old charity-bin type garments.) What Piriel meant was that people should concentrate on top-quality classic styles in colours that could be teamed together. When I moved to the apartment, my appearance would be transformed . . .

There were dozens of other odd jobs listed, but I went upstairs to say hello, knowing it couldn't be avoided much longer. I had to put up with being kissed by the Trentons, but luckily managed to dodge Joan Cordrice, who was crammed in between some of the packing cartons. (Being hugged by her was like being smothered in a feather doona.) The card-group members weren't repulsive or anything, it was just that, like Aunt Dorothy, I preferred to keep my distance from people. (With her it was only shyness. I wasn't particularly shy, but I always felt awkward if people touched me, not knowing how to react. Piriel wasn't into hugging or kissing, either, which was most likely why we got on so well.) Apart from hugging each other every time they met, and also being absolutely boring, Aunty Nat's mates were harmless enough. In fact, they were all very kind. Last year Derek Trenton had made a sleeping basket for Horace. He made it as occupational therapy while recovering from his hip-replacement operation. And Sheila, his wife, sewed a quilted lining for it, even though she had bad arthritis in both hands. Arthritis never kept her away from Aunty Nat's card nights, though. Right now they were all playing a round of Trivial Pursuit as a warm-up for cards. Everyone tried to talk me into joining in. They'd do that whenever I happened to be staying with the aunts on one of their card nights, but I usually got out of it by saying I had homework to do. (Elderly people always trustingly believed that excuse, even when it was school holidays.) Because it seemed rude to scoot right downstairs again, I sat on the arm of the couch for a little while and watched the game.

Mr Woodley seemed to be making himself very much at home for someone on their first social visit. He even jumped up to fetch a cloth from the kitchen when Aunty Nat's charm bracelet sent someone's drink flying. (As usual, Aunty Nat looked totally overdressed in a flowery skirt and matching top, a white lace cardigan, and big rose earrings clamped on her ears like pink barnacles.) Not only did Mr Woodley mop up the table, but he insisted on moving the chairs around so Aunt Dorothy, whose drink it was, could sit next to him and have more room. It wasn't even necessary, I thought. She'd been comfortable enough at the far end of the table.

'Don Bradman!' Aunty Nat yelled. (Every time she landed on a sports question, she'd say Don Bradman or Muhammad Ali, which seemed to be the only famous sporting names she knew.)

'Well, I guess we could pass it, seeing the question was about cricket,' Sheila Trenton said. 'Now, Joanie, you landed on a green one, didn't you? Green – that's science kind of things; oh yes, here it is. What word describes the sort of gold found in river sand?'

'I know it, just give me one little minute! Allusive?'

'Warmish, but not quite right, dear.'

'Alluring, then!'

'Getting warmer . . .'

'It's *alluvial*,' I interrupted.

'So it is, but no one can say gold isn't alluring, too. What say we pass it, seeing Joan got the first syllable right?'

It was really pathetic, the bending of rules that went on in their warm-up games of Trival Pursuit! Luckily, Eileen Holloway arrived then, late as usual, which meant an excuse to escape by hopping up to let her in. (It also meant having another wrinkled old cheek pressed against mine and not being able to do anything about it.) Eileen floated into the living room to join the others. Aunty Nat's famous card group, relocated to its new premises at Avian Cottage, Parchment Hills, was in full swing. I'd done my duty as far as politeness went, and could now go downstairs with a clear conscience and finish off the jobs on my list. Except it didn't seem a very fascinating way to spend the evening . . .

I hung about in the hall, listening to the cheerful din, feeling rather out of things. Which was stupid. I knew that if I'd actually *wanted* to play Trivial Pursuit or cards, all those kind old dears would have been delighted. But because I'd already practically snarled at poor Aunty Nat for suggesting it, it seemed too embarrassing to go back in there. I glanced at the phone, wishing I could ring Dad. It was depressing when people could only talk to each other with a lot of fussy details about time zones. (Actually, Dad always preferred to call *me* when he was overseas, not the other way around. That was so I wouldn't disturb him if he was busy or catching up on sleep after a heavy work schedule.) It seemed ages since he'd last phoned. It would be nice, I thought, if he didn't just keep vanishing for weeks on end. It must feel good to have a parent who was around permanently, in the same place. Then you wouldn't have to built up a relationship all over again, each time you met.

'Sarah, would you mind checking Eileen's car?' Aunty Nat called. 'She can't think if she locked up properly. Oh, and while you're about it, just make sure the headlights aren't still on, dear.'

Eileen's car was parked outside in the road (she was a bit nervous about getting herself in and out of driveways). The curtains weren't drawn in the Ryders' living room, and you could see in. I suddenly remembered Corrie's invitation from yesterday, about watching videos. That invitation had been genuine; you could tell by the way she'd said it. She'd made it sound the easiest thing in the world, just a matter of turning up and banging on their front door. Maybe I could *still* do it, even if I only stayed for half an hour or so. I could use their phone to let Aunty Nat know where I was, so she wouldn't think I'd been kidnapped out on the street. It wouldn't be hard to invent some convincing reason why I hadn't gone out with Piriel, either, as I'd said I would. Corrie would just say, 'That's okay, it's great you could make it after all, Sarah. Come in and meet all my friends.'

It wouldn't happen like that, though; it never did at school. Somehow, I just didn't seem to have any talent for mixing with other kids. It was a mystery, because I didn't know what I was doing wrong. Once, Tara McCabe had even yelled at me, 'I bet if there's such soppy things as guardian angels, the one you've got keeps begging for a transfer!' (We were out visiting a museum exhibition at the time. Tara had sneaked off and bought a bag of crisps, eating them behind Mrs H.'s back. She'd offered me some, but I'd reminded her about the rule of not eating in public places while wearing school uniform.)

I moved further along the footpath, to the Ryders' gate. From there you could see the whole of their living room, and what everyone was doing. They had their Christmas tree decorated already. There were four sleeping bags arranged in a semicircle facing the television set, but no one seemed to be watching properly. Corrie's friends were racketing about all over the place. Mr Ryder came in with a handful of ice-cream cones. He sat down to eat one, too. Corrie did something to the footrest on his reclining chair and his feet shot up in the air. He hit her with a cushion. They all hit him back. Mrs Ryder brought in a big plate of cocktail sausages, which everyone ate with their hands. Corrie put on a different video which nobody watched, either. They were all too busy chattering to each other and mucking around.

I felt like a traveller passing through a strange town late at night, gazing through a lighted window at a party. There was no way I'd fit in with that crowd of girls who already knew each other. I didn't belong down there. Slowly, I turned around and went back to Avian Cottage. In the front hall, I looked at the phone again. Piriel Starr was different; I never got on *her* nerves. She'd said right from the start that she knew we were going to get along just fine. I picked up the phone, then dialled her number . . .

'Guess what, Aunty Nat!' I cried a few minutes later, bursting in on the serious business of the card night, which was a mind-numbing jackpot game that went on for ever and ever. 'Piriel said if I meet her tomorrow at the Moreton Shopping Centre she'll help me choose something to wear to the wedding! Oh, and by the way, Eileen left her car keys in the ignition. Here they are.'

'Thank you, dear. And that's very thoughtful of Piriel; it should be a nice outing for you,' Aunty Nat said.

The card-group members didn't have to ask whose wedding it was – Aunty Nat had kept them up to date on every little detail since Dad and Piriel first met. Eileen Holloway said gooily, 'What a sweet way to start off the new year, having a family wedding! Have you ever considered holding the reception here at Avian Cottage, Nat? I think garden settings are always *so* romantic.'

Aunty Nat glanced up from her hand of cards. (It was always quite easy to tell from her expression if she'd been dealt good ones. She would have made a terrible secret agent.)

'That darling little porch out the front would be just perfect for bridal photos,' Eileen added. 'Almost as lovely as a gondola in Venice.'

Aunty Nat laid down her cards in full view, not even realising everyone could see she had the joker. 'Now why didn't I think of it myself?' she cried. 'Not just the reception, but having the whole caboodle here – the marriage ceremony and everything! It would be a bit of a rush, but I don't see why I couldn't get everything ready in time. It would be so much nicer than a registry office! That's what they were planning, would you believe – a registry office, then going on to some restaurant straight afterwards. It's certainly not *my* idea of a proper wedding. I wonder if I could talk them into changing their minds –'

'But Piriel's already made her own plans,' I said quickly, trying to stop her getting carried away. There was nothing Aunty Nat liked more than buzzing around arranging things that involved a lot of eating. 'You can't just –'

'They could have the actual ceremony down in our little summerhouse,' Aunty Nat prattled on, as though she hadn't even heard. 'Catering wouldn't be any problem, either. If the weather's nice enough we could use the deck . . . though maybe not with all those greedy rosellas hanging around. A kind of buffet thing set up inside might be better. And I could make the wedding cake, too!'

'But Piriel wasn't even planning on having one . . .'

'Even if I do say so myself, my cake decorating is every bit as good as a professional's. You remember that beauty I rustled up for your niece's twenty-first, don't you, Joanie? Once Christmas is over we'd have a few weeks clear run. Ed, could you perform some kind of miracle and get all the repairs and painting done by early February?'

'No worries,' Mr Woodley said. 'Just let me bung in those new stumps first before I start on any fancy-work, though, Nat. Can't have the old place sliding off down the hill with a mob of wedding guests inside.'

First-name terms already, I thought darkly, eyeing him across the card table.

'Let's see, now,' Aunty Nat said, starting to jot things down on one of the score pads. 'There's the stumps, then painting the house inside and out, summerhouse ditto, new gravel for the paths . . . Sarah, maybe I should delegate this list to you, dear. You're always such a dab hand at them.'

'You'd better attend to it, Aunty Nat. I've got homework to do,' I hedged, because that was one list I really didn't want to get involved with. It would be an *insult* to Piriel, suggesting that she might like to have her wedding at a dumpy old house like Avian Cottage!

5

· · · · · · · ·

Christmas list ideas

Aunty Nat: New recipe file. Flowery notepaper. New Gilbert and Sullivan cassette (yuk!). Silver lyrebird bracelet charm she's been admiring in Parchment Hills jeweller's window (aaaargh!!!).

Aunt Dorothy: Pair of proper slippers. (NB So she can throw out those grungy old plastic thongs!) Something for the garden – plant, gardening gloves? OR – book on how to quit smoking once and for all!

Darling Horace: Gourmet sardines. Smart new collar. Big packet of Kitty Krunchies.

Card-gang sharpies: Sheila Trenton – 4711 cologne; Derek Trenton – box of soft fudge suitable for denture wearers; Joan Cordrice – spectacles chain; Eileen Holloway – potpourri.

Dad: Tie? Socks? Hankies? Travel alarm clock? (No

good; he prefers wake-up calls. Plus there's already an alarm-clock thing on his watch.) Nice pen? (But he's got *heaps* of them.) What do you buy for a person who already *has* everything?!

Piriel: ?? What *do* you buy for a person who already has everything?!

Christmas cards

Mrs H. at school.

Belinda Gibbs, Tara McCabe, Marnie Kydd. (But all three of them still owe *me* cards from last Christmas!)

Corrie Ryder ??

· · · ·

'Tagging along wasn't *my* idea,' Aunt Dorothy said mildly. 'Nat didn't want you going all that way on public transport by yourself. She feels responsible. Anyhow, I've got Christmas shopping to do, so I'll probably beetle off once I've handed you over to Piriel.'

I was relieved to hear that. Piriel wasn't expecting anyone except me, and might feel humiliated to be seen with someone else who looked so scruffy. (Aunt Dorothy *had* actually rustled up a pair of ladderless pantyhose, but then spoiled the effect by bringing along a gross shopping bag made of camouflage canvas.) I still had some Christmas shopping of my own, too. If we finished looking for clothes early enough, I thought, Piriel might be able to help me find a wonderful Christmas present for Dad. Presents for him were always difficult. Every year I racked my brains, but usually ended up getting hankies, ties or socks. Piriel had the whole day off work; she'd said so on the phone. It shouldn't take more than an hour to choose something to wear to the wedding. She'd probably be the first one to suggest that we spend the rest of the day Christmas shopping together.

'If you've forgotten anything, there won't be any time to go back for it,' I said impatiently, because Aunt Dorothy had just backed the car out of the drive, then stopped again. 'Piriel's expecting us at ten *on the dot*. We've got to meet her in the lower mall next to the –'

'Next to those automatic-teller machines. Yes, I already know, dear. You've mentioned it quite a few times already. And you can stop fussing, because we're just waiting for that little girl from next-door. Nat told her mother we could give her a lift.'

'Corrie Ryder? What a nerve, cadging lifts all over the place when we hardly even know them!'

'Where she's going is just round the corner from the Moreton Centre, so it's not even out of our way.'

'Their living room's messy. I saw through the window last night when I was checking Eileen's car. They even had food sitting around on plates on the *floor*. Well, I'm just glad *I* didn't have to eat any of it!'

'Sarah, don't be such a toffee-nose. The Ryders seem very nice people.'

'Their house isn't. It's even more run down than Avian Cottage.'

'They probably can't afford to do it up. They've put all their money into buying a plant nursery, and good luck to them. Corrie's a pleasant enough kid. When she brought that goat over before breakfast . . .'

'Meg's a *dumb* name for a goat,' I said, turning a little red.

'. . . I really think you might have shown some interest. She was just about to show you how to tether it, only you'd already nicked back inside. And it doesn't matter what that goat's called, as long as it gets rid of some of the blackberries.'

I could think of plenty of reasons for not showing more interest in Corrie Ryder. While we waited, I went over some of them in my mind.

1. She was a pain in the neck.

2. She had a laugh like a kookaburra's.

3. She poked her nose into things that weren't any of her business.

4. She was tactless about people's names (ie Piriel's).

5. If I was too nice to her, she might get the idea I actually wanted to be her friend.

Corrie came hurtling out, not even shutting their gate behind her. She didn't close the door of the car properly, either, so we had to stop further along to fix it. She was off to this place where you could climb walls studded with rocks. Even though she had a grazed knee from her last visit there, she sounded as though she could hardly wait to have another try. (I felt amazed that anyone could not only *want* to do something like that, but also pay to get in!)

'It's *awesome*! I'll probably go again before Christmas,' she said. 'Want to come along if I do?'

'Thanks all the same, but I don't think I'm going to have any spare time before Christmas.'

'There's a big water slide up in the lake park. That's great, too. Now it's swimming weather, maybe we could –'

'I'll be very busy,' I said, cutting her off short.

Aunt Dorothy, who was being decidedly irritating this morning, butted in with, 'Get along with you, Sarah. You sound like a company director. I could always drop you and Corrie off at the lake park and pick you up again later. Or the wall-climbing place, if you'd rather have a shot at that.'

'I'll have masses of cards to send out. And Christmas shopping to do, if I don't finish it all today,' I said curtly. Corrie's exuberance was *already* driving me up a wall! It was hot in the car, but the air-conditioning was out of action. (It had been like that ever since Aunty Nat let Scott and Cameron tune it instead of having it done at a proper garage.)

'My Christmas presents were a breeze this year,' Corrie volunteered. 'I just bought a lot of old books at the junk shop, then hollowed out the pages with a Stanley knife. You make a kind of little pit for hiding valuables, but it still looks like an ordinary book. I thought I'd fill the cut-out spaces with gold chocolate coins, so everyone will get the general idea.'

'Goodness, I remember making one of those when *I* was a kid!' Aunt Dorothy said. 'I'd forgotten all about it. Except I got into a row over mine, because I'd used a library book by mistake. But what a super idea for Christmas presents! It shows you must have loads of imagination.'

I felt a little twinge of something that felt almost like jealousy. It wasn't just because of the compliment about having loads of imagination, though I couldn't help thinking that Aunt Dorothy had never said anything like that to *me*. It was more because she was chatting so easily to Corrie. Usually she didn't strike up conversations with people she'd just met. If she was collecting me from school on Fridays instead of Aunty Nat or Dad, she preferred to wait in the car until I came out with my bag. She said it saved time, but I knew it was to avoid any stray parents, teachers or kids. But now she and Corrie Ryder were crackling away at each other like a house on fire. They were talking about gardening, of all things! Corrie not only sounded as though she knew quite a lot about it, but was actually *interested*.

'If it's ideas for hedges you're after, you should check out our nursery,' she said. 'Dad's got all sorts of hedge plants.'

'Does he have jacaranda trees, too? I *love* them.'

'If he hasn't got any in stock right now, he can always order you one. And if you like azaleas . . .'

It almost felt as though I was the one being given a lift instead of Corrie. I stopped listening and concentrated proudly on what kind of outfit to buy for the wedding. It would have to be *very* special, something that would make Dad and Piriel pleased to introduce me to their friends. Something that made me look glamorous and interesting . . .

When we dropped Corrie off at the indoor rock-climbing place, she waved goodbye from the entrance, but I didn't react until she'd gone inside. My mind was still full of the wedding. I kept seeing myself, beautifully dressed, mingling with all the guests and knowing *exactly* what to say to each one. Putting last-minute touches to Piriel's hair before the official photographs. Piriel and Dad insisting that I should be included in all those photographs. Offering to get people fresh drinks, and not spilling one drop. Except Avian Cottage somehow kept appearing as the backdrop for all those delightful images, which was perfectly *ridiculous*!

'That was kind of rude, Sarah, not waving back to

Corrie,' Aunt Dorothy remarked, turning left for the Moreton Centre.

'You just missed the arrow lights,' I said distractedly. 'We're going to have trouble finding a parking spot.'

We cruised around all the car-park levels twice. Aunt Dorothy wasn't aggressive enough to thwart people stealing spaces from right under her nose. I began to chew at a fingernail, but even when we finally wangled a space, she stopped to look at a bank of native plants. Heat blasted across the enormous car park like dragon's breath, but I still couldn't hurry her along. She took no more notice of heatwaves than she did of being punctual for appointments! I might as well have tried to shove Mount Kosciuszko another metre further along to the left.

Piriel, dressed in white and looking as cool and unruffled as iced milk, swept aside my flustered apology about being late. She even smiled at Aunt Dorothy as though it was a pleasant surprise to have an extra person on our shopping trip. (She didn't flinch at the sight of the camouflage bag, either. The way Piriel managed that, I saw with keen interest, was to glance at it once, then pretend it wasn't even there.) And most graciously of all, she wouldn't hear of Aunt Dorothy going off on her own.

'Oh, you *must* stick around while we shop,' she said. 'Sarah will need shoes and a bag to go with the new dress, and it will be more fun deciding all that between us. Pity it happens to clash with the pre-Christmas rush, though. Aren't the decorations *vile*, all those ghastly chiming bells strung up everywere? They only seem to be programmed for "Joy to the World". I thought I'd go crazy while I was waiting, having to listen to that over and over again.'

I'd been just about to mention how pretty the bells looked, and felt glad I hadn't. (I didn't mention the heralds with their gold trumpets, either, in case Piriel thought they were ghastly, too.)

'I had an idea about your dress, Sarah,' she said. 'How would it be if we search for a pattern instead of buying a ready-made one? The summer fashions this year all seem so ugly, specially for your age group. It would be much better to choose a pattern and some lovely material, and I'll make it in time for the wedding. We want you looking your very best, don't we?'

I felt elated, knowing that anything made by Piriel would turn out to be stunning. She made a lot of her own clothes, and they always looked wonderful. The shop she took us to had one whole large section set aside for patterns. Piriel began to flick through the heavy albums, as though she knew exactly what she was hunting for. I glanced at Aunt Dorothy, suspecting that she really *would* have preferred to beetle off on her own. She was always bored by anything to do with clothes.

'They've got a craft section over there,' I said, inspired. 'Maybe you might find a Christmas present for Aunty Nat.'

It wasn't such a brilliant inspiration. Aunt Dorothy used the aisle behind the counter as a direct route to get there. One of the busy shop assistants had to shoo her out from underfoot, and it was a disaster when she finally reached that craft section, anyway. She set her bag down on the floor, and someone immediately tripped over it. Straight after that she knocked over a stand of embroidery kits, flattening somebody else. Piriel, with great presence of mind, called her back and asked her to go over to the far side of the shop to see what they had in the way of small white buttons. She made it sound as though it was a vital mission, but winked at me secretly as Aunt Dorothy trotted off. It felt wonderful, the two of us sharing a conspiracy, left in peace to look at patterns together.

'Between you and me, I'm rather glad Nat didn't decide to come along, too,' Piriel said. 'Poor old Dosh is *quite* enough to be getting on with, but at least she never pretends she knows anything about clothes . . . Aha, search over! Something in this style is what I had in mind for you.'

I inspected it doubtfully. It wasn't really the sophisticated sort of thing I'd been imagining on the drive down from Parchment Hills. In fact, it seemed a little on the young side for someone my age, vaguely like something you'd see on an old-fashioned porcelain doll.

'Now it's just a matter of finding the right material,' Piriel said. 'Which shouldn't be any problem. They always have a great range here – that's if Dorothy hasn't managed to demolish their whole stock by now. Let's go and find something *really* gorgeous for you, sweetie. Didn't I tell you this would be fun?'

Piriel had perfect taste and knew all about fashions, I thought. There was no need to feel anxious about my new dress. I followed her through the shop, hoping that people would see we belonged together. But I didn't like to get *too* close. Piriel had a strong invisible boundary, which somehow made getting close to her seem like an intrusion. The aunts didn't have any boundaries to speak of, even Aunt Dorothy with her ship-in-a-bottle daffiness. It always felt the most natural thing in the world to help Aunty Nat fasten a necklace, rub sunscreen lotion on Aunt Dorothy's back at the pool, get splinters out for them if they couldn't find their reading glasses. But Piriel was different, and the zone around her somehow demanded respect. Aunt Dorothy, however, suddenly bounced into it, flourishing a long roll of buttercup-yellow material as though she was conducting an orchestra.

'Look what I found!' she beamed. 'It's on special, too, marked down half price. Not that I've got any clues about girls' dresses, but don't you think the colour's just –'

Piriel didn't care for it at all (maybe because Aunt Dorothy accidentally swiped her on the chin with the roll). She said that yellow always reminded her of thick banana custard. Aunt Dorothy seemed a little

81

downcast and didn't offer any more suggestions. They weren't necessary, anyway, because Piriel chose an ivory-coloured cottage print, scattered delicately with lilac flowers. She was quite definite about it.

'It will suit Sarah *perfectly*,' she said. 'She's such a quaint little article.'

I felt the tiniest bit doubtful again, because I wasn't sure I was a cottage print kind of person. (Or a quaint little article, either, for that matter!) But trusting her judgement, I was happy to let her pick out shoes, too, after we'd bought the dress material. Aunt Dorothy didn't come with us on the rounds of shoe shops. We lost her at the first one, and had to backtrack to where she was riffling through a stand of books outside a newsagency. (She'd heard somewhere that detective stories made good reading for long plane trips, so that's what she gave Dad every Christmas. I never had the heart to tell her he didn't like them.)

'The rest of this business might take a while. We must be holding you up, Dorothy, with the Christmas shopping you wanted to do,' Piriel said tactfully. 'If you'd like to get on with that now, we could all meet again in the café next to the fountain, let's say in about forty-five minutes. Would that be the best plan – what do you think?'

It was remarkable, the smooth way she could get rid of someone and sound polite about it at the same time. Aunt Dorothy loped off quite obligingly, and we were able to look for shoes with no interruptions. The ones Piriel liked best were very plain ivory leather, with a narrow buckled strap.

'You don't think they're maybe a bit too much like . . . well, like little kids' party shoes?' I asked hesitantly. 'And they're *terribly* expensive . . .'

'They're just right for the dress, Sarah,' Piriel said. 'So is this nice little matching bag I've just found on the other counter. And not to worry about how much it all comes to. I'm paying by credit card, and Brett will reimburse me for whatever I've spent. We can't have you turning up at our wedding wearing cheap trendy rubbish, can we, honey? There, that's everything taken care of, so now we can go and treat ourselves to a delicious lunch. I think we deserve it.'

Aunt Dorothy was ten minutes late meeting us at the café, and when she did show up, knocked over the sugar bowl by dumping a large wooden doorstop on the table. The doorstop was a goose wearing a painted bonnet and apron.

'Christmas present for Nat!' she said triumphantly. 'Seeing she's so keen on bird things because of the house name . . . oh, that reminds me, did you pass her message on yet, Sarah? About the wedding reception being at Avian Cottage?'

It wasn't nearly as awkward as I'd thought (maybe because that goose was so hideous nothing else seemed quite as bad). Piriel dealt with it skilfully.

'That's generous of Nat. Tell her I'm very grateful

for the offer, but I've already made a tentative booking at a restaurant one of my friends owns.'

'Bet they can't make wine trifle as good as Nat's,' Aunt Dorothy said. 'People always have trifle at weddings, don't they?'

'Well, not *everyone*, not these days, anyhow. The restaurant might be closed for renovations early February, though, that's the only hitch. Look, don't go damaging Nat's feelings or anything. It's not that I'm *completely* ruling out the Avian Cottage idea, but I don't even know if it's feasible or not, do I? It's not as though I've actually seen the house yet.'

(I stored 'feasible' away in my mind to look up in the dictionary later, perhaps to use myself when I found out what it meant. Piriel's words always sounded somehow exactly right, like pearls graded in order of size.)

'I hope no one feels offended that I haven't been out to visit yet,' she added lightly. 'I would have given you a hand moving in, of course, if we hadn't been so frantically busy at work. But Nat's very kindly invited me for Christmas dinner. So I'll be able to have a good look then, won't I?'

I gazed out into the mall, at the crowds of shoppers under the canopy of silver bells. There was a queue outside Santa's castle near the fountain. (Last year Aunty Nat had herself photographed sitting on his knee, using printed copies to send to everyone as Christmas cards. I'd been with her, pretending not to know her while she was lining up with all the little kids, although everyone else seemed to find it amusing. Santa had even given her a lollypop out of his sack.) I looked at the goose doorstop again, knowing that Aunty Nat wouldn't think it was hideous at all; she'd probably adore it. Maybe I could find a bird thing for her, too. The rest of the day would be terrific, getting caught up in the excitement of Christmas gifts now that the clothes were out of the way.

'I guess everyone must be secretly cursing the timing of this wedding,' Piriel said. 'It won't give people much chance to recover from all the usual demented Christmas and New Year fuss, I'm afraid. And Dorothy, I didn't even think to ask what *you're* planning to wear to it! For all I know, Sarah's material might clash terribly with your best dress. Or are you lashing out and buying something new? We could do that now, if you like. Sometimes it's useful to have another opinion. Sarah and I could hover around and give expert advice.'

It was clear that Aunt Dorothy hadn't given any thought at all to what she'd wear for the wedding. She muttered in a confused sort of way that she supposed she'd just borrow something of Nat's when the time came, taking the hem down so that it would be long enough. But I could tell she was scared stiff at the idea of trying on clothes with Piriel hanging around and giving expert advice.

'Aunt Dosh already has a nice blue dress she's hardly ever worn,' I said quickly.

'And anyhow,' Aunt Dorothy added, sounding more assertive than she usually did. 'I haven't got time to mess around looking at blooming clothes today. I've still got more Christmas shopping to do. So has Sarah.'

Quite suddenly, I found that I could hardly wait to start. Tracking down nice gifts for people would be so easy with Piriel there to help me. Specially Dad's one. She might even ask my advice on what *she* should buy for people. Corrie Ryder, I thought happily, was more than welcome to her old carved-out book safes. It was just plain scungy giving people homemade junk gifts like that! The rest of this shopping expedition was going to be absolutely –

'Don't remind me about Christmas shopping!' Piriel said, putting down her empty coffee cup. 'I loathe and detest the whole silly business. If you don't mind, I'll just take myself off now and leave you two ladies to it. Oh, mustn't forget the dress stuff! I'll get it cut out, Sarah, then we'll arrange a time for a fitting later on. Give my regards to Nat. And tell her I'm sorry I haven't had a spare moment to see the hacienda . . .'

I felt flat when she'd gone. Somehow the day hadn't been quite as enjoyable as I'd expected, and now the rest of it would be reduced to nothing more than plodding around the shops with Aunt Dorothy. Even the prospect of Christmas-gift shopping didn't seem terribly exciting now. It was just a silly, demented fuss, as Piriel had said. A waitress came and took the used plates away. Because Piriel was so tidy in everything she did, there wasn't as much as a crease in the tablecloth to show that anyone had actually been sitting there opposite us. There was just a lingering fragrance of perfume from when she'd leant across to say goodbye.

'What's a hacienda?' Aunt Dorothy asked.

'I think it's Spanish for house.'

'Is it? Fancy that. You know, I wasn't very peckish before, but I see they've got trifle on the menu. How about you, my quaint little article?'

I suspected some kind of dig at Piriel, but because Aunt Dorothy's eyes were as innocent as a baby's, I just ignored it. (That 'quaint little article' business made me feel uncomfortable, anyway.) After that, although she insisted on going outside into the sweltering car park for a cigarette first, the rest of the afternoon wasn't really too bad. Aunt Dorothy was never in a hurry, so I had plenty of time to look at things carefully before deciding what to buy. There was one crazy moment, staring at ties and initialled hankies, when I actually thought of making Dad one of those burglar-proof book safes like Corrie's. They might be scungy junk, but somehow seemed more *fun* than anything on the display racks. But then I remembered the security system at the new apartment, and realised how pointless it would be going to such a lot of trouble for something that wouldn't even be used. I ended up getting him socks again because I just couldn't think of anything else.

I'd had the same problem on Father's Day. He'd been away for that, too. It wasn't just the difficulty of finding something interesting, either. Giving someone a gift after the reason for it had passed somehow felt like a disappointment. Just for once, I thought, it would be great if he was home for a special occasion. Such as Christmas . . .

Aunt Dorothy, who'd seemed quite happy to plant herself nearby and daydream while I was choosing those socks, woke up when we went to buy gift-wrapping and ribbon.

'Brown paper and raffia isn't Christmassy – it's just *weird*,' she objected. 'You do get some barmy ideas, Sarah.'

'It's not a barmy idea. Piriel used exactly the same on a house-warming present she bought for someone. It's artistic.'

'This other stuff is what *I* call proper Christmas paper. Now, let's see, should I pick the holly or the snowmen? The holly one's shinier. Oh, and a big hank of tartan ribbon plus some of those loopy bow things you stick on top . . .'

I started to point out that tartan ribbon would look awful with the holly paper, but shut up. It didn't really matter what trimmings Aunt Dorothy chose. No one could ever work out just what she did to make all her presents resemble bundles of fish and chips!

'Now for the toy department,' she said eagerly. 'I always like that part of the Christmas shopping best.'

The toys were for all the grandchildren belonging to the card-group members. The aunts always gave them presents at Christmas and on their various birthdays.

Watching Aunt Dorothy choose this year's toys, it suddenly hit me that it was a bit sad. She and Aunty Nat probably felt left out of things when the Trentons, Joan Cordrice and Eileen Holloway started boasting about their grandchildren at the card nights. The aunts didn't even have any children of their own, let alone grandkids . . .

'Let's see – that's Sheila's lot all ticked off, except for little Joshua. This robot might be just the thing for an eight-year-old. I wonder what it does –'

'Don't fiddle with the buttons!' I warned, too late.

The robot began to zap everything in sight, and neither of us could work out how to switch it off. Aunt Dorothy panicked and dropped it. It nipped out through the door, beeping loudly and heading for the escalator. A sales assistant had to run to head it off. (It was just as well, I thought, that Piriel *hadn't* come along with us, because she would have found the whole thing undignified.)

'Don't you *dare* play with anything else,' I hissed, too late again. Aunt Dorothy was already tugging a helicopter from the next shelf, avalanching everything stacked below. I put it all back and followed her into the next aisle, dealing with other minor avalanches on the way. It was hard, though, not to get caught up in her enthusiasm at finding things for all those little kids. *I* started to enjoy it almost as much as she did. But after it was finished and we went back out into the mall, I began the serious business of looking for Piriel's gift.

Tracking down the right item proved to be impossible.

Everything seemed just too ordinary, and Aunt Dorothy's ideas weren't much help. All she could think of was perfume, but I knew I'd never be able to afford the sort Piriel wore.

'How about a T-shirt?' she suggested. 'They always come in useful.'

'Piriel doesn't wear T-shirts. She says they lose their shape after a few washes.'

'That's when they start to feel comfortable, after they lose their shape. What about a scarf, then? Can't say I'm keen on the dopey things myself; they just seem to get caught up in bus doors and everyone gawks at you. But Piriel's probably never been on a bus in her life, so she might like one. Look, there's a whole stand of them here.'

'Piriel only likes *silk* scarves.'

'Excuse me for breathing!' Aunt Dorothy said. 'Well, there's no sense in getting het up about one little present. The way you're carrying on, anyone would think it's one of those army obstacle courses. How about if you sleep on it a bit more? You might get a brainwave before Christmas. And it's time we were getting back to the hacienda, anyway, signorina.'

It seemed the best thing to do, I thought reluctantly. Piriel's gift, being so important, really *did* deserve a whole day set aside for it specially. (But first I had to set Aunt Dorothy right by explaining that 'signorina' was actually Italian, and that she should have said 'señorita' if she was trying to be so clever.)

6

· · · · · · · ·

Irritating things about Parchment Hills

1. All the neighbours natter at you.

2. So do the shop people.

3. Everyone is *totally* interested in everyone else's business. Examples:

- newsagency lady: 'How did your aunty's hair colour turn out this week?'

- hardware man yelling across the street: 'Tell Ed I got those sprockets in for him, love!'

- postman: 'I see you've got a postcard from your dad in the States.'

- woman walking dog past Avian Cottage: 'How are the renovations coming along?'

4. Birds squawking around the house all day long.

5. Not being able to unpack the rest of my things because of moving again soon.

· · · ·

'Dinner, tickets to that big Christmas production of the *Nutcracker* ballet, plus a night at a posh hotel,' Aunty Nat said. 'It's not very often you win such a decent prize in a raffle. I told the Ryders to go off and enjoy themselves and not worry about a thing. Corrie should be comfy enough staying here overnight, even though it's only a mattress on the floor.'

'She could just as easily sleep up here on the couch.'

'That wouldn't look very hospitable. She's the same age as you, so *of course* I had to put you both in together. I do wish you'd be a bit more friendly.'

'Horace won't like having a stranger around.'

'You can't call Corrie a stranger when she lives right next-door. Horace is over in their yard half the time, anyway. You could take a hint from that, Sarah . . .'

'You should call him back when he wanders off. And another thing, he ought to be kept in the bath-room when the workmen are here, even if he *does* get stuck under the tub. It's better than sealed up inside a wall, like yesterday.'

That had happened while Aunt Dorothy and I were at the Moreton Shopping Centre. Ed Woodley took part of the staircase wall down to check the electrical wiring. When it was done, he replastered the gap, which was when poor Horace started mewing. They'd had to cut a new hole to rescue him.

'Horace took all that in his stride,' Aunty Nat said airily. '*You're* the one having kittens about it, not him. As a matter of fact, he's been scratching around ever since, trying to get back in again. And I'm afraid it won't be much use shutting him up in the bathroom tomorrow, either, dear. They're starting the new plumbing in there. The whole floor will have to come up, and it's going to be a jackhammer job. Whoever was responsible for laying that slab didn't use thick enough concrete, you know. The bearers along that side will have to be replaced because of water seepage, not to mention the studs and probably some of the noggings. Just as well Ed and his mates can attend to everything. Oh, what a treasure that man is!'

Although Aunty Nat was rattling off technical terms like a builder's apprentice, I knew she'd only picked them up over cups of tea with Ed Woodley and his mates. And after tomorrow she'd most likely be showing off with a lot of new plumbing terms, too! I was *sick* of the renovations, anyhow; it was like camping on some development site. It was getting so you couldn't even use the loo without making an announcement first. (Otherwise you couldn't be sure a face with a mouthful of nails wouldn't suddenly pop up outside the window.) Aunty Nat didn't seem to mind any of the inconvenience. She'd even gone ahead and set up our Christmas tree amongst the clutter of paint tins, ladders and tools in the living room. Christmas was only two days away, and it wouldn't be very nice for Piriel, I thought, expected to visit us in such a mess. Even though I kept hinting to Mr Woodley that we'd be having an important guest for Christmas dinner, he didn't bother hurrying anything along. He just made jokes about it. Such as Michelangelo hadn't moved his scaffolding every time the Pope dropped into the Sistine Chapel for an eyeful.

'There's Corrie at the door now,' Aunty Nat said. 'She might like to help us decorate the tree.'

We were quite capable of decorating our own tree, I thought indignantly, letting Corrie in. As well as her overnight things, she'd brought along a plate of homemade rum balls, a stack of gardening books for Aunt Dorothy, and a tape of Christmas songs from all around the world, sung by some choir her mother belonged to. That tape was so scratchy you could hardly tell if they were singing carols or 'Waltzing Matilda', but Aunty Nat thought it would be lovely background music while we decorated the tree. (We didn't let Aunt Dorothy help with that when she came in from watering the garden. She was on her honour to just sit and watch every year, otherwise there were always too many casualties.) The tree took up most of the evening, because Aunty Nat had collected dozens of ornaments over the years. Suddenly I wasn't too keen about someone else, even if it was only Corrie Ryder from next-door, seeing those ornaments at close range. *Particularly* the cardboard reindeers and sleigh, which was something I'd made way back in kindergarten. It looked more like crocodiles harnessed to a fork-lift.

'It's about time we turfed this old thing out,' I said self-consciously.

'We just couldn't!' Aunty Nat said, sounding horrified. 'The tree wouldn't be the same without that on top.'

'People always have *stars* on top.'

'We sometimes don't at our place,' Corrie said. 'This year we put up a Santa Claus. He's got this red nose and when you tweak it he goes "Ho, ho, ho!" It's kind of cute.'

Corrie seemed to have just as bad taste as Aunty Nat, I thought, watching in disbelief as she admired the ceramic elves Eileen Holloway had given us last Christmas, a string of miniature plastic plum puddings, a fairy with an inbuilt battery light installed in its wand, and a whole flock of robins (new this year).

'Tough luck Horace is so scared of birds,' I said, hoping Piriel wouldn't notice them too much when she came. 'He might have done a pretty good demolition job on these, otherwise.'

'Don't be cheeky about my little robins, Sarah,' Aunty Nat said. 'I happen to think they're delightful. Buying them seemed a nice way to mark our first Christmas at Avian Cottage. And be careful of those angels; they're no longer exactly in their prime.'

That was an understatement, I thought, sorting out the gold flying angels which had been ancient even before I went away to boarding school. (Originally there'd been half a dozen of those simpering angels. Now, though, there were only five, because of Aunt Dorothy's carelessness with a cigarette lighter one Christmas.)

'All this old junk can stay packed up next year,' I told Corrie. 'The aunts won't even need to set up a tree. Piriel will probably want to have Christmas at the apartment instead, so they'll come in and visit *us*. I can just imagine the fantastic dinner she'll have, too! *And* her tree decorations. Probably something very simple, but all colour-coordinated, so when you walk in the door –'

'I can't see us not having a tree, dear, even if the family get-together's held in town from now on,' Aunty Nat said cheerfully, but her expression somehow didn't match. I realised, feeling guilty about it, that I might have upset her without meaning to. She'd always gone to a lot of trouble to make Christmas special. Rattling on about how great it would be with Piriel in charge must have sounded ungrateful.

'Well, this year's one is certainly coming along a treat,' Aunt Dorothy said, as though she was trying to smooth over my lapse. 'Even if it's not what you'd call colour-coordinated. Mind you do decent knots for all those baubles, kids. The darn things always seem to bounce off if I as much as *look* at them.'

'It's having a stickybeak at presents does that,' Corrie said, grinning at her. 'That's how my dad always gets sprung, too.'

'Glad I'm not the only guilty one. Here's hoping everyone will like what I got them this year. I'm not very cluey at buying stuff for people. Somehow I never seem to get it quite right.'

I didn't like to agree out aloud, even though it was true. Last year she'd bought me a squashy black velvet hat. It rained the first time I wore it, and black dye came gushing out like an oil well. (I couldn't go anywhere for a couple of days till my hair changed back to its normal colour.) Other things came to mind: a zebra trinket box with a spring-loaded lid like a set of teeth (nerve-racking to open and shut); a box of silver-coated paper and envelopes, but no matter how hard you pressed, writing just wouldn't dent the surface. (Somehow, though, I could never make myself turf out any of her dud presents.)

'It's the thought that counts, Dosho,' Aunty Nat said, spraying the poor tree lavishly with Santa Snow as though it was some kind of fertiliser. 'I'm sure everyone will be happy enough if whatever you've bought them still happens to be in one piece when they take the wrapping off. Piriel's the one who's hard to buy for. I've racked my brains, but I honestly can't think *what* to get her.'

'How about a brooch?' Corrie suggested. 'That's what I got Mum last year. A leaf brooch, it was, because of buying the nursery. Dad reckoned I should have bought her a gag instead for egging him on.'

'Piriel doesn't wear brooches,' I said, secretly wiping off some of the Santa Snow. They'd had it plastered all over the Christmas trees at the Moreton shopping centre, too. Piriel had remarked how silly it was, using snow as a decoration for hot Australian Christmases.

'Oh drat, are you *sure*? I thought everyone liked them,' Aunty Nat said. 'Maybe something for the new flat, then. I could always give Eileen a ring and see if she still has some of those unicorn bookends.'

'Piriel wouldn't like those ghastly bookends. It's an *apartment*, anyway, not a flat.'

'What's the difference?' Corrie asked inquisitively.

'Not a great deal, except for the price,' Aunty Nat said, frowning at me a little. 'And I'll have you know, young lady, Eileen's unicorns sell like hot cakes as fast as she can dab the glitter on their collars. *All* her ceramics do. I was thinking about buying a set of her Camelot wine goblets as a wedding present.'

'Piriel wouldn't like those any better than the bookends. Anyway, Dad says it's a *crime* to serve wine in anything except proper glasses.'

'There goes that idea, then. Oh, and speaking of the wedding, you haven't told me much about your dress pattern and material yet. What with Horace just rescued out of the wall when you came back from Moreton yesterday, we never really got around to it.'

It was odd, but I suddenly developed a mental

block, unable to remember more than sketchy details. Aunt Dorothy's attempts weren't much better. 'It was kind of old-fashioned, like the little girls wore in that TV series about the early American settlers,' she said. '*Little Town on the Prairie* or whatever it was called. Sarah used to watch it when she was small. She liked the log cabin they all lived in.'

'*Little* House *on the Prairie*,' I said, displeased. 'And it wasn't *anything* like those dresses, Aunt Dorothy!'

'Well, that's what the pattern reminded *me* of. The material did, too. It was all-over violets or something.'

'You're making it sound yuk! And it wasn't, it was *excellent* material!'

'Well, the shoes and bag are nice enough,' Aunty Nat said. 'Though I would have preferred something fancier myself. Maybe you could tizz that handbag up a bit, Sarah. I've got a sparkly buckle that might do the trick.'

'*No!* Piriel has perfect taste and those things are just right the way they are!' I snapped, then wished I hadn't in front of Corrie Ryder.

She looked as though she never growled at *anyone*. No matter how irritating people were, she'd probably just sit there with that sunny expression plastered all over her face. And it wasn't surprising she was so unflappable, I thought crossly. *Anyone* would be if they'd always lived in a boring little place like Parchment Hills where nothing exciting ever happened! Even so, nobody had any right to look so relaxed all the time, to act so *contented* with life and everything in it. She even thought the five gold angels were beautiful, and suggested dangling them from the light fitting as a special feature. (Just as she'd pushed in earlier by fixing a crooked branch on the Christmas tree. She'd splinted it with a chopstick and fuse wire, before *I'd* had the chance to think up a remedy.)

'Those angels have always gone in a line along one wall . . .' I began, just to remind her she was only a visitor.

'What a good idea! They'd look so pretty underneath the light,' Aunty Nat said at the same time. 'Grab a chair, dear, and I'll pass them up one at a time.'

I wasn't sure which one of us she meant, but as I'd had quite enough of Corrie raking in praise for good ideas, I got there first. It wasn't a job to improve anyone's mood, though. Cotton had to be looped through each halo, and Aunty Nat, who wanted a kind of mobile effect, kept making me shorten or lengthen the threads. Negative thoughts kept fluttering about inside my mind, one for each angel I hung:

1. I might look really *stupid* in a dress nearly down to my ankles, with little violet flowers all over it.

    ['Be careful with this one's wings, Sarah,' Aunty Nat said. 'Some of her feathers seem to be moulting.']

2. Piriel, just *possibly*, might have made a mistake choosing a pattern and material like that.

['Oh, thank you, Corrie; what a bright girl you are! I would never have thought of holding feathers in place with hair spray.']

3. Those new shoes definitely *were* the tiniest bit like little girls' party shoes.

    ['Should be some hair spray on my bedroom dressing-table, dear, left-hand side next to the hand lotion . . .']

4. How was it that some kids could walk into a place, immediately feel at home, and everyone automatically liked them straight off ?

    ['You should have come over for dinner, Corrie, as well as staying overnight. It wouldn't have been any trouble at all. We just had ham and salad, anyway, because of the heat. There's still plenty left over in the fridge, so if you get hungry in the middle of the night, please feel free to help yourself. Sometimes it's very hard to get to sleep in hot weather like this.']

5. How would *I* get to sleep with someone I hardly knew in the same room? (Sharing with Tara McCabe at school was difficult enough! For instance, she wasn't the least bit grateful whenever I tidied up before room inspection. So we wouldn't lose marks, I'd dash around to pick up her dropped socks from the floor, smooth both our bedspreads,

hang up her blazer, put her slippers neatly under the bed where they were supposed to be kept – and I'd never get any thanks for it! She usually just slouched in the doorway glaring at me.)

'All done,' Aunty Nat said. 'Those sweet little angels almost look real floating around up there. Now all we have to do is find the pine wreath for the front door, and we're all set for our very first Christmas in Avian Cottage!'

'I have a feeling I might have seen it somewhere or other downstairs,' Aunt Dorothy said drowsily. 'Which is where I'm heading now, if nobody minds. I'm ready to hit the sack. Yanking out all that ivy today was hard work, even though Ed Woodley gave me a hand with the worst bits.'

Aunty Nat, noticing that it was after ten, suggested bedtime for *everyone*, but first she followed us downstairs to hunt for the lost wreath. (It was slung up behind the bathroom door, being used by Aunt Dorothy as a temporary towel hanger.) After Aunty Nat found it, she had a sudden inspiration about louvred doors for my wardrobe. I was secretly relieved when she began to fuss around with a tape measure, because it meant I didn't have to make stiff conversation with Corrie while we were getting ready for bed. She didn't seem to feel ill at ease, though. She was chattering away to Aunty Nat like an old village gossip.

'. . . no need to go all the way down to Moreton.

The local cinema gets all the new movies at the same time they do. *Plus* there's a half-price double feature every Monday.'

'Really? Well, I'll certainly take advantage of that.'

'And the best video shop is the one next to the newsagency. It's got a bigger range than the arcade one.'

'Thanks, dear. Next time we hire videos, I'll check it out.'

'The Wilkinsons own it. They live out near the reservoir, and Dad's going to landscape their backyard when they get around to deciding what they want. Mr W. likes traditional gardens and she likes bush ones. Tim Wilkinson – that's their kid – delivers the local paper in this street. He's in the archery club I belong to.'

'Sarah, wouldn't *you* like to try archery? It would be a nice hobby for the holidays,' Aunty Nat said, but I just made a sound that could mean yes, maybe, or no way.

'There's plenty of other things to do up here as well as archery,' Corrie said, still waffling on about Parchment Hills. 'They've got canoes for hire up at the lake this year. The Quigleys run the kiosk up there. I take their dog for a walk every afternoon, because they don't get home till late in summer. They live down the hill in Number Eleven. Oh, and I'd better tell you the best place to park if you ever have to go to the hospital in an emergency. That hospital car park's only tiny, so it's always full up. But if you drive further round the corner into Ganan Street, there's a . . .'

None of it interested me; Parchment Hills wouldn't even be part of my life very soon. I gave my pillow a good thump, thinking how easily Corrie Ryder seemed to slot into everything, as though the whole area was just an extension of her own house! Perhaps she saw the whole world like that, too. If she ever found herself adrift on a raft, no doubt she'd feel completely at home *there*, and probably just look forward to the experience of eating raw fish! And the way that prize traitor Horace had been slurping up to her from the moment she'd set foot in Avian Cottage, you'd think *she* was raw fish!

'Well, I'd better let you girls get some sleep,' Aunty Nat said, tucking in my bedspread, brushing back my hair, kissing me on the forehead, then giving me a lit-tle pat on the cheek.

For as long as I could remember, that had been a kind of ritual whenever I stayed with the aunts. Aunty Nat's hands always smelled of jasmine lotion. She kept jars of it all over the house, so she could pamper her hands every chance she got. (Eileen Holloway made the lotion as a ceramics sideline.) It was babyish, but being tucked into bed last thing at night was some-thing I quite often missed when I was back at school. Once, I'd secretly taken a jar of that hand lotion back with me, and when I felt miserable at night, I'd take off the lid to smell the jasmine.

'Night, Sarah. And thanks for letting me stay at your place,' Corrie said, after Aunty Nat had switched off all the lights and gone away upstairs.

'That's okay,' I said politely, though it wasn't anything to do with me and had just happened because Aunty Nat was being neighbourly over the fence. Horace, who'd parked himself on Corrie's mattress, stirred at the sound of my voice but was too lazy to jump back to where he rightfully belonged. (Which was in his sleeping basket next to *my* bed.)

'You'll have to come over and sleep one night at our house. Only if you *want* to, of course. Mum reckons you probably get sick of being around other kids all the time because of boarding school.'

As soon as she came out with that, I knew they'd been talking about me behind my back.

'Not really,' I said swiftly. 'I've got stacks of friends there, and I *never* get tired of them. As a matter of fact, I'd be staying at my friend Tara's place these holidays, only I thought I'd better stick around here to help my aunts get settled in. Tara lives way out in the country. We would have gone horse riding every day.'

'There's a riding-school place in Parchment Hills. If you feel like it sometime, maybe we could –'

'Thanks, but I'm going to be flat out for the whole holidays. It's just as well I *didn't* go off to Tara McCabe's, with all the things I've got to do before school starts again. There's the wedding –'

'I just had a good idea for that. You could tie a white

ribbon on Horace and have him sitting by the front door when the guests show up!'

'The wedding reception's probably not even going to *be* here. Aunty Nat would like it, but nothing's decided yet.'

'But I thought it was kind of *definite*. I mean, Aunty Nat's getting a loan of some garden urns from our nursery. She's already told Dad what she has in mind; cherubs on the sides, I think it was. They're for white flowers to go on the porch steps.'

'It's going to be in the *city* somewhere,' I said, annoyed about her saying 'Aunty Nat' casually like that, as though she had some personal connection. 'Most likely at this restaurant Piriel's friend owns. And as well as the wedding, there's another reason why I won't have time for archery or any of those Parchment Hills things you were talking about. I'll be too busy helping fix up our apartment ready for us to move in. Lorraine will want me there when she's choosing furniture and stuff . . .'

'Lorraine?' Corrie asked, yawning. 'Who's Lorraine?'

'I meant *Piriel*. And maybe we'd better not chat any more with Aunt Dorothy just down the hall. We'll be keeping her awake,' I said, although Aunt Dosh always fell asleep the minute she got into bed and stayed that way until morning. (Even a huntsman spider waltzing across her face probably wouldn't have woken her up.) It was just that the stupid blunder of mixing up those two names made me want to pull the sheet over my head.

Lorraine was someone Dad was married to before he met Piriel. It had happened in London, when they were both working over there on a long-term project. She wrote to me a few times, saying how sorry she was that I'd missed out on the wedding, and how much she was looking forward to us all being a family when they came back. And that Dad said to pass on the news that we'd be getting a terrific house somewhere, maybe near a beach. I'd told everyone at school that I probably wouldn't be there next term, that I'd be moving. The marriage had only lasted seven months, though, and they'd come back separately. I'd never even *met* Lorraine.

Corrie Ryder had fallen asleep, I could tell by her breathing. Trying to get there myself, I began a list of phrases, using the last word to make a following one. Christmas tree, tree house, house guest, guest room, room to move, move over, over the hill, hillbilly, billy tea, tea for two, two's company three's a crowd . . .

Usually it was quite a good method for falling asleep. Sometimes, though, the list petered out and you couldn't get anywhere with it. I tried some more.

All systems go, go for your life, lifeblood, blood is thicker than water, water pipe, pipedream, dreamland, land on one's feet, feet first, first off the mark, marksmanship, shipboard, boarding school, school friend, friendless . . .

They didn't seem to travel anywhere, either. I came up from under the sheet and gazed at the stars instead. Now that Aunt Dorothy had cut the ferns back from around the window, you could see a great dazzling sweep of night sky. There might be a book about astronomy in Parchment Hills library; maybe I could learn how to find the different constellations. Though there wasn't much point, really, not when I was moving to the city so soon. There were so many other lights in the city, you wouldn't be able to see the stars clearly. This end room had a magnificent view of them, but it would be wasted on Aunt Dorothy if she changed her mind and shifted in here when I left. She didn't lie awake at night. Corrie Ryder seemed to have that same ability to fall asleep with no trouble at all. It must be a handy knack, I thought, to be able to put yourself to sleep and dodge your thoughts for a while.

7

. . . .

Piriel

P is for polished perfect personality possessing poise
   plus.
I is for impressive intelligent individual.
R is for remarkable real estate agent running rings
   round the rest.
I is for idol!
E is for excellent, elegant executive.
L is for leading lady.

Sarah

S is for sulky, stupid show-off.
A is for article (quaint little), and awful nails.
R is for really really *really* boring.
A is for *average* at *all* things.
H is for hateful horrible hideous hair; hard to get
   along with; hopeless.

. . . .

109

'It's a wonder you didn't invite his plumber mate while you were about it. Not to mention that other guy who helped him with the new wiring.'

'Well, I did, actually, but they've got families of their own,' Aunty Nat said. 'For your information, Miss Scrooge, Ed Woodley *hasn't*. How would you like to be by yourself on today of all days, eating something heated up in a microwave? *And* no one to chat to because of not liking to intrude anywhere on Christmas –'

'That didn't stop him intruding on *us*.'

'It's not intruding when you've been asked. Same as Piriel's been asked, so instead of acting uncharitable about poor Ed, you can make yourself useful and try ringing her. She really ought to be here by now. Oh, and you might check the table first, just to make sure I haven't forgotten anything.'

She hadn't. All the glasses had ivy twined around their stems and the rims frosted with eggwhite and castor sugar. There were red Christmas-theme embroidered tablemats, candles in snowball holders, a gingerbread-chapel centrepiece with another candle inside to light up the coloured windows, and place-tags made of star biscuits glazed with each person's name in green icing. It looked very festive, but I suddenly saw it through Piriel's eyes. She might think it was all ridiculously over-the-top, like a float in a parade. A parade float, complete with visiting clown.

I frowned at the biscuit that said 'Ed', tempted to scrape off the icing and pipe his name over again using strong mustard. No risk of *him* being late – he'd arrived ages ago, and was outside in the garden talking to Aunt Dorothy. He was doing most of the talking; I could see them both through the dining-room window. She was just nodding every now and then, most likely feeling bored to death. If Aunty Nat was going to invite strangers at Christmas, I thought resentfully, she should have at least made sure they had some stylishness about them. Piriel would be bored to death by Ed Woodley's conversation, too.

I dodged through all the renovation muddle in the hall and dialled her number. No one answered, which must mean she was already on her way. Going back through the living room, I retied the bow on the present I'd bought for her. Aunty Nat hadn't liked my choice of raffia cord and plain brown paper, either, and she'd offered me some of the partridges-in-pear-trees wrapping paper which was her own choice this Christmas. But I was *proud* of how artistic my presents looked, so I'd turned it down. Ed Woodley had also brought gifts for everyone, putting them under the tree when he'd arrived. They were latticed all over with sticky tape, just as incompetently as Aunt Dorothy's. Even though he'd also brought a bottle of champagne, I didn't approve of the way he was muscling in on our Christmas!

As far back as I could remember, there'd always been this leisurely annual ritual at the aunts' place. We gave each other one little token present at breakfast, but the proper ones were saved for after lunch. Morning was for going to church, with everyone joining in the carols, and when we got home, I'd help Aunty Nat get the enormous meal ready. It always ended with coffee and cake around the tree, and opening the presents seemed to take up the rest of the afternoon. Later on, Aunty Nat would make a wonderful supper, and we'd have a traditional game of Scrabble. Spread over the whole day and evening like that, Christmas with the aunts felt unhurried and somehow gentle. The best Christmases, of course, were the ones when Dad was home, though they really didn't happen very often.

'Piriel's not answering,' I said, going into the kitchen where Aunty Nat was doing some complicated things to a sauce. 'I hope you didn't draw one of your weird maps and post it off to her! People end up getting lost when they rely on those maps. You should have just said to look it up in the street directory – though she might think Lawson Avenue's a short cut if she does that. She won't know it's blocked off because they're doing roadworks.'

'Don't distract me about anything now, there's a good girl,' Aunty Nat said absently. 'This recipe's as tricky as the Bermuda Triangle. Scoot out and tell the others we'll be sitting down in about twenty minutes. Piriel's sure to turn up by then. Nobody ever misses out on Christmas tucker if they can help it.'

I went outside to deliver the message, making a detour first to see if Piriel's car was in sight. There was always a chance that she'd mistaken some other old house in the street for Avian Cottage. It was *full* of shabby old houses just like Avian Cottage, and no one seemed to bother about keeping their gatepost numbers in good repair, either. Ours was faded away to nothing, though Aunty Nat said there wasn't much sense repainting them. (She'd already ordered custom-made ones from Eileen Holloway, with the thirty-three shaped to look like flying swallows.) I hovered around the gate, filling in time, then thought that might seem immature when Piriel arrived. It would look as though I could hardly wait to see what she'd brought me for Christmas. So I went around the back to tell the others that Aunty Nat's feast was nearly ready.

They were inspecting the summerhouse. Probably they'd headed down there to get away from the racket next-door, I decided. The Ryders were having a Christmas barbecue. It had been going on since mid-morning and was getting louder by the hour. They were Corrie's grandparents, aunts, uncles, cousins and so on; Mrs Ryder had told us over the fence that they held a big family get-together every Christmas. There seemed to be hordes of noisy little visiting kids, but the grown-ups were making just as much din. They all seemed to be chasing each other with water-pistols or something. I climbed down to the summerhouse, thinking how strange it must be to have as many relations as that, enough to fill up a huge back garden.

'We've just been round the side looking at your courtyard, Sarah,' Aunt Dorothy said. 'A standard rose might be nice for that centre bed, with alyssum as a border. Or maybe you'd rather have –'

'I'd better leave all that up to you. It's not as though I know the first thing about plants,' I said quickly, not wanting to get involved. Having a little private garden outside my bedroom door might be something to miss when I moved to the apartment. I sat out there sometimes, before anyone else was awake. One morning a butterfly had settled on my arm. There was a shrub of pink flowers that looked like butterflies, too. They had a beautiful scent, and I'd been meaning to ask Aunt Dorothy what they were called . . . but there was no point, really. Avian Cottage was only a house I'd visit every now and then with Dad and Piriel. 'First course is just about on the table,' I added, hearing a car and ducking back up the path to the front gate.

It was somebody else's car, and whizzed straight past without stopping. When I went inside, Aunty Nat said Piriel had just rung saying to start without her, because she'd been held up unexpectedly. I didn't really enjoy the meal, although the food was delicious. I didn't feel much like talking, either, though the others didn't notice because they were all chattering about the improvements to Avian Cottage. Various reasons why someone could be late for a special occasion like Christmas dinner kept niggling away in my mind:

1. They could have a flat tyre.

2. They could have more *serious* car trouble.

3. They could have been involved in some kind of road accident and Aunty Nat didn't want to say so because of spoiling Christmas . . .

But Piriel always kept her car in perfect condition, and was too good a driver for car accidents. Besides, Aunty Nat didn't seem upset about anything, either. She was even giggling at Ed Woodley's pathetic jokes, and so was Aunt Dorothy, who usually had to have jokes explained to her patiently phrase by phrase. She somehow looked different today, I thought, then realised with amazement that not only had she bought herself a new shirt, but had also borrowed Aunty Nat's turquoise earrings! Usually she hated earrings. The turquoise made her eyes very blue. She looked quite pretty, and I felt pleased that she'd made an effort to smarten herself up because of Piriel coming.

Piriel, however, didn't arrive until we'd reached the coffee stage. I flew to let her in, so I'd have the chance to warn her in a hurried whisper about Ed Woodley being invited and what a disaster he was. Before opening the door, I took off the fur-trimmed red cap I was wearing. It suddenly felt silly, even though a festive decoration for everyone was another one of our Christmas traditions. (This year, Aunty Nat's was a holly necklace, Aunt Dorothy's a Santa Claus badge, and Ed Woodley looked like an absolute idiot with plastic pixie ears clipped on over his own.) Piriel apologised for being so late, explaining that some important people she and Dad knew had invited her to call in, and she hadn't been able to leave as early as she'd hoped. Aunty Nat was disappointed that she didn't want any of the food saved for her.

'Thanks all the same, but I've spent all morning having to nibble poolside snacks,' Piriel said. 'At the moment I really can't face anything except strong black coffee.'

'Try some of Nat's cake,' Ed Woodley insisted, helping himself to another slice. 'It's powerful enough to hoist anyone up on their feet belting out all the verses of "Jingle Bells".'

Luckily he could only remember the chorus, though Aunty Nat's fruitcake really *was* something to sing about. I hoped he'd restrain his greediness so there'd be enough left over for Piriel when she'd got her appetite back. For the moment, she just seemed to want to sit peacefully and drink her coffee. Ed Woodley, though, started telling a long story about how he'd once spent Christmas day trapped inside someone's roof. He was there doing emergency repairs, they'd gone off to visit friends, and the ladder had slipped out of the manhole leaving him stranded. Piriel looked so sophisticated it made me squirm to watch her being forced to listen to anything so tedious. Even in plain black pants and a sleeveless black top, she somehow managed to look glamorous. Aunty Nat kept offering her a silver star to pin in her hair, which also had the effect of making me cringe. (Piriel, although she accepted it in the end, left it lying casually on the coffee table.)

She'd also been wearing black (and looking just as glamorous!) in a photo I'd shown around at school. I'd felt so proud telling everyone it was my new step-mother-to-be, but Tara McCabe, obviously jealous, said Piriel would come to her senses before she actually married someone who had a dorky kid like me. I didn't think Piriel felt I was a dork. There certainly wasn't any hint of it in her voice when she interrupted Ed Woodley's next story (about someone's waterbed falling through the floor once when he was restumping), to ask if she could see over the house.

'Sarah, would you like to do the honours?' she asked. 'Maybe a quick look at the garden first, only just from the deck, if you don't mind. The heels on these shoes aren't really designed for the great outdoors.'

Although it was me she asked, it turned into a big production number with *everyone* trailing out on to the deck carrying drinks (and in Ed Woodley's case, another great hunk of cake). Aunty Nat pointed out the summerhouse, as proud as though she'd built it with her own hands.

'Isn't it the darlingest thing you ever saw?' she said. 'We're all dying to see how it looks once it's painted, but Ed has to finish all the main jobs first. And down that other path there's a little ornamental pond, though it's all clogged up with weeds now. Dosh is 'going to clean it out and put in some waterlilies.'

'The garden's absolutely charming,' Piriel agreed, and to my surprise added that Avian Cottage was charming from the outside, too. (I'd really thought that she'd hate it on sight and consider it just plain funny looking.) 'You might be overcapitalising with all the renovations, though,' she said critically. 'It's such a long way out of town, I doubt if you'll get your money back when you want to sell. Now if it was in the inner suburbs, you'd be able to ask a fortune.'

But the aunts didn't *want* to sell, I thought, feeling confused. It was their dream home. Aunt Dosh had planted a walnut tree, and they took years to grow; she sang to herself when she worked in the garden. Aunty Nat had started making a set of flamingo tapestry cushions for the living room, to match the wallpaper frieze.

'Inner suburbs? Who in their right minds would want to live *there*? That's yuppy territory, that is,' Ed Woodley said, blundering into the conversation. He almost brought it to a standstill. Piriel gave him the kind of look you'd give to someone jostling in a queue, and Aunty Nat suggested quickly that we go back inside and see through the house now. Piriel handled that part well, completely ignoring the stray tools and equipment strewn all over the place. She didn't even flinch at my magpie courtyard door, the carved eagle on the landing, the parrot wallpaper in the dining room, or the swans in Aunty Nat's upstairs bathroom. While we were in that ensuite she rinsed her hands, and dried them on the embroidered guest towel laid beside the basin. With all the visitors who'd trailed in and out of Aunty Nat's place over the years, I couldn't remember *anyone* ever using the guest towel! It must be wonderful, I thought, to have such poise and confidence.

'Well now,' she said when we were all back in the living room. 'I can see that having the wedding here might be rather nice, Nat. Such a *lovely* setting . . .'

Aunty Nat began to beam like a sunrise.

'You've just about convinced me, too, I think,' Piriel said. 'It might be an excellent idea, though I'm just wondering if the renovations could actually be finished in such a short time. I can see Mr – sorry, I've forgotten your name – has done an enormous amount of work already, but . . .'

'The new stumps are in,' Ed Woodley said, sounding affronted. '*That's* the hard yakka part. Everything else is just a doddle from now on.'

'Then if your offer stills stands . . .' Piriel said, smiling at Aunty Nat, who was the only person I knew who actually clapped her hands when she was overjoyed about something. (Though I wouldn't have put it past Corrie Ryder, either.)

To celebrate, Aunty Nat poured everyone a glass of Ed Woodley's champagne, including a half one for me. She looked so happy that I felt quite pleased, too, about the plans being altered. More than pleased, really. Avian Cottage suddenly seemed *right* for such a special event, much more fitting than a registry office.

Dad had married Lorraine in a registry office. This wedding should be different; it should have a completely different beginning to it.

'Now that's all settled, we can get on to passing the presents around,' Aunt Dorothy said hopefully, because although her own gifts to people were usually such catastrophes, she was like a little kid about watching them being opened.

'Oh yes, Christmas loot,' Piriel said, taking an envelope from her bag. 'Here you are, Sarah.' At first I thought it was just a card, but then realised it was her actual gift to me. Inside was a brochure and a term's membership for a children's theatre workshop in the city. 'Every Saturday afternoon, starting in February,' she explained. 'Normally there's quite a long waiting list, but I know someone who's a tutor there. She was able to do a bit of string-pulling, so you're a very lucky girl. I thought it would give you something to do on weekends when we all move to the apartment.'

'Maybe they'll put on a play and we can come and watch you act, love,' Aunty Nat said, but I gazed down at the brochure, not knowing quite what to say. I'd never been any good at acting, or even particularly interested in it. At school the closest I came to it was being in charge of props and costumes. (The drama-coordinator there said I was the most reliable person she'd ever met for making sure a bowl of fruit was onstage in its correct place at the right time.) The idea of going to a proper acting workshop every Saturday afternoon made me feel nervous. It sounded *dedicated*, or something. All the other kids there would probably be *brimming* with talent.

'I see you're still nibbling away at those nails,' Piriel said reproachfully. 'Maybe I should have bought you a manicure set as well! I can't *possibly* have a step-daughter with bitten fingernails, you know. Brett would just have to put you up for adoption.'

I could have died from shame. Luckily, Aunt Dosh, outdoing herself in clumsiness, knocked over the milk jug, which wasn't even anywhere near her.

'Sorry,' she said. 'It's splashed on Piriel's nice shoes, too. What a shame.'

'*You're* the one who should be put up for adoption, Dosho,' Aunty Nat scolded, but they both smiled at me and I felt a bit better.

'Thanks, it's a fantastic present,' I said to Piriel, handing over the one I'd bought for *her*. It was a bronze paperknife made like a little sword, and had cost more than all my other Christmas shopping put together. (Surprisingly, I'd found it in a secondhand shop in Parchment Hills.) Piriel said it was so adorable she'd keep it in full view on her desk at work, where everyone else could see it. I would have been embarrassed to clap my hands with joy, like Aunty Nat, but for an instant I almost felt like it. The gift had been a success. It was clear that Piriel didn't want to risk losing it in the tidal wave of paper beginning to swamp the living room, because she rewrapped it immediately, then tucked it away in her handbag.

She'd bought beautiful scarves for the aunts. Aunty Nat put hers on straightaway, as she always did with anything new, but Aunt Dorothy managed to trail hers into a cup of coffee, so it had to be rinsed immediately and laid flat to dry. Aunt Dorothy seemed more enthusiastic about the five-thousand-piece jigsaw puzzle I'd bought for her, anyhow. I hoped Piriel wouldn't think I was mad buying something like that for an adult, then saw that she wasn't really watching. She was glancing discreetly at her watch. For one uneasy moment I thought she must be totally bored with *all* of us, not just Ed Woodley. But then she caught my eye, smiled brightly and said she'd just remembered that the most important gift, my present from Dad, was still in her car if I'd like to run out and fetch it. It turned out to be a notebook computer, which he'd asked her to buy in time for Christmas.

'That game software was a gimmick from the shop,' she explained. 'I suppose one game won't matter, but just bear in mind, Sarah, that this particular computer isn't meant to be a toy. The general idea is to help you get ahead with *school work*.'

'Well, whenever she wants to quit school, she can come and work for me,' Ed Woodley said. 'I'll take her on as foreman. Sharp as a knife, she is, when it comes to figuring out how many rolls of wallpaper. We'll corner the renovations market in no time, won't we, young Sally?'

'*Sally?*' Piriel remarked, raising her eyebrows at me in private.

'Yep,' Ed said carelesssly. 'She doesn't mind, except for shooting me a greasy look about it every now and then.'

'Sarah's planning to stay at school for a good many years yet,' Piriel said, as though he'd actually meant the foreman thing. '*And* do well enough to get a place at university one day, we hope.'

I felt slightly uncomfortable, almost guilty. The best that could be said about my academic record was that I somehow managed to keep up. Dad often said he hoped I'd choose law or medicine as a career, but I personally didn't think I was cut out for anything like that. Not if my school marks were anything to go by. Scraping through, not failing, just average, keeping up with the others – it wasn't good enough. Not *nearly* good enough for someone who was having vast sums of money spent on their education at an expensive private school . . .

'Oh, thank you, how thoughtful! Did you make them yourself?' Piriel was saying politely about her present from Aunty Nat. (You couldn't have guessed from her voice that she probably detested being given three frilly aprons with heart-shaped pockets.) Ed Woodley's present for Aunty Nat was almost as bad; a wind chime made of tinkly plastic birds, each one a different colour. Aunty Nat didn't have to try to be tactful; anyone could see she *loved* it.

'It's *beautiful*, Ed!' she cried. 'But I just meant you to bring yourself along, not a whole swag of goodies. There's already that lovely feathery tree you gave Dosh.'

'A jacaranda,' Aunt Dorothy told Piriel shyly. 'We planted it before lunch, down the back where the garden runs into the bush block. I've never grown a jacaranda before.'

Piriel pointed out that it might not flourish, because they were meant for warmer climates. I was impressed all over again by how much she knew on so many different subjects. Ed Woodley, however, cut her short by passing us each one of his sticky-taped presents, a box of pencils for me, and a key ring for Piriel.

'That's very kind of you,' she thanked him. 'It even has my initials.'

'They stuck in my mind from hearing Sally talk about you so much,' he blurted, which I found embarrassing (although I suspected I *did* rattle on rather a lot about Piriel in general conversation). 'Only I've just thought of something – you're looking at the lame-brain of the year right now! That thing won't be much use to you in a few weeks' time, will it? After your wedding, I mean . . .'

'S for Starr?' Piriel said. 'Being married won't make any difference about that. I'll still be keeping my own surname. Must keep up with the times, and it's easier for business purposes, anyway.'

I felt an odd little sensation, like tripping over an

unexpected step. Without even thinking about it, I'd just assumed Piriel would take our family name when she married. I'd even written it out to see how it looked – Piriel Radcliffe, Brett Radcliffe, Sarah Radcliffe – a whole, complete, newly minted family. Aunty Nat was wearing a slightly disapproving expression, I noticed, as though she thought Piriel was being far too modern altogether. But that was just such an old-fashioned attitude, I realised indignantly. Piriel was *perfect*. She shouldn't have to change her name for any reason, not if she didn't really want to.

'I'm itching to get started on this jigsaw puzzle,' Aunt Dorothy said. 'It's beaut, Sarah – all these cats are the spitting image of dozy old Horace on one of his more intelligent days. Anyone else want to have a bash at it? Bags me the edge bits, though.'

'Dosho, I do think that could wait till tomorrow,' Aunty Nat objected. 'Sarah's being very good about keeping her computer for later, so I think you might show some restraint, too.'

'I wish I could ring Dad up right now,' I said. 'I want to thank him for it.'

'Better wait for him to ring here, pet,' Aunty Nat said. 'He wasn't sure if he'd still be at that same hotel today. Don't worry, there's still plenty of Christmas left for him to get a call through. There's tea to come yet, and then our game of Scrabble. We *always* play Scrabble after the presents and everything . . .'

But Piriel said that although it sounded a cosy way

to wind up the day, she'd prefer not to join in. In fact, she added, she'd really have to be making a move now, because there was still someone else she had to visit.

'Friends, but potential clients as well,' she said. 'I *think* I've just about convinced them that art deco is *exactly* what they want. Can't risk a sale by neglecting possible clients at Christmas, can I? Oh, and speaking of real estate, the apartment's just about ready if you three ladies would like to have a look. It's not painted yet, but practically everything else is done. I would have liked to show you over it myself, but I'm going to be tied up for the next few days. How about if I leave this spare key and you can have your own private viewing?'

'Tomorrow?' I asked excitedly. 'Would that be okay, Aunty Nat, if we went in tomorrow?'

'Actually, some of Brett's pals wanted to see through it then,' Piriel said. 'It might be rather a tight squeeze if you all happened to turn up together. But any other day after that would be fine, and you could just drop the key in at my office afterwards. Sorry to put you to that inconvenience, but I'll need a spare key for the interior decorators. Once you've had a good look at your room, Sarah, let me know what you'd like in the way of wall colour and curtains. Oh, and another thing – you look very sweet today, just like a little Christmas snowflake.'

So although she had to leave before Christmas was properly over, I wasn't left standing on the front porch crushed with disappointment. She'd *noticed* I was dressed all in white. Maybe she even realised it was meant as a compliment to the way she'd been dressed when we'd gone shopping at Moreton. And now there was this other thing; seeing over the apartment and then choosing curtains and paint for my new bedroom – it was as though Piriel had given me an extra, very special present before leaving. She trusted my judgement!

8

. . . .

Personal items (ie junk!) unsuitable for the apartment

(To be thrown out, recycled, given away to people, left behind at Avian Cottage. And no getting choked up or any stupid last-minute excuses!)

1. Eileen Holloway's kitten paperweight.

2. Zebra trinket box with the lid like clacky teeth.

3. Treasure Island money box.

4. Alarm clock with dragon feet.

5. Teddy bear. (?)

6. Cracked mug with photo print of Horace on it. (??)

7. Cedar chest. (???)

8. All my old picture books from when I was little. (????)

9. Raggedy old circus bedside mat, from before I went away to school. (?????)

10. Roll-top desk. (??????)

(Maybe work on this list later. It's too hard deciding. There's no hurry, anyway.)

Interior-decorating ideas for room at apartment

1. Ship's cabin look: walls lined with pine, bunk bed with drawers underneath, brass lantern lights, maps. (Could also hang onto Treasure Island money box, then.)

2. Everything all white-on-white: white walls, white carpet – maybe not with Horace around, new white towelling bathrobe. (Could paint roll-top desk glossy white.)

3. Geometric look: each wall a different colour (yellow, blue, orange, green), modular furniture all slotted into each other, striped canvas blind instead of curtains, polka-dot carpet. (Make zebra trinket box a display feature.)

4. Exotic, mysterious Oriental look: gold or red walls, low bed like a platform heaped with satin cushions, paper-lantern lampshades, Horace's basket relined with red satin, big swaggy curtains with tassels. (Maybe *keep* dragon alarm clock?)

5. Sky theme look? Curtains like the ones Belinda Gibbs had at her house . . . YES! Cloud material curtains, white or pale-blue walls, stick-on stars for ceiling, cloud-shaped cushions, fluffy white sheepskin mat (could still keep circus one under-neath), decorate roll-top desk and cedar chest with sun stickers. (Could store all the other dis-card-list things inside chest, so I wouldn't have to throw anything out after all!)

. . . .

Ed Woodley came straight back to work after Boxing Day (probably because he couldn't last any longer than that without the din of power tools). Yelling to make herself heard, Aunty Nat suggested that it might be an ideal time for the rest of us to inspect the apartment. I rushed to get my camera and the new memo book I'd bought specially for interior-decorating ideas.

On the long drive into town, I added more things to the list I'd started for my room at the apartment. I liked the sky theme best. It seemed an inspired choice for life in a tower, further up in the air than most people lived, and it had come about from suddenly remembering Belinda Gibbs's bedroom curtains. I'd noticed them at her birthday party. (Actually, what I'd noticed most of all was that the hems had been chewed to tatters by her dog.) The material had been pale-blue cotton printed with white clouds. I'd phoned her yesterday to ask where they'd bought it, and although she'd apparently just popped out on her rollerblades somewhere, her mother gave me the shop address. It was in the city, and Aunty Nat had promised we could buy some today if they had any left.

I could hardly wait to tell Piriel about that brilliant sky theme, hoping she might be impressed enough to ask for my help in decorating the rest of the apartment! And every time we had visitors there, she might make some comment about it. First she'd take them to look at my room and say, 'Sarah planned this all by herself. She has such *wonderful* taste for someone her age. It's a pity I can't show you the little paperknife she gave me for Christmas, but it's on my desk at work. I keep it out on display, because it adds such a special touch to the whole office.'

Thinking along those lines meant I could just about bear listening to the soundtrack tape which Eileen Holloway had given the aunts for Christmas. It was called *Rainforest Birdsong*. They played it all the way into town, only switching it off when we turned into St Aloysius's multilevel car park. Aunty Nat said it would be more convenient to leave the car there and catch a tram, because she'd forgotten to ask Piriel what the parking situation was like up near the apartment. That wasn't the real reason, though. Aunty Nat *always* used St Aloysius's when she had to go to the city. I suspected it was because she thought God would keep a personal eye on a church car park, zapping anyone who tried to break into the cars. While she was whisking up through all the levels to find a vacant spot, I kept my eyes firmly closed. It wasn't as though Aunty Nat was a bad driver, but her running commentary tended to make you feel on edge.

'Now what's that big galoot trying to do?' she murmured vaguely. 'Is he backing out or just straightening up the wheels? Should we wait just in case he's leaving; what do you think, Dosh? Oh drat, he's stepping out and locking up! Goody goody gumdrops – *there's* one. Oops! It's just a little space full of fire hoses. What a *rude* driver behind us – Santa must have given him a new car horn for Christmas! If I wasn't a lady, I'd make a finger sign out the window. Maybe I could squash in next to that red van, though we'd all have to hop out my side because of the concrete pillar . . . no, better not risk it. These ramps always seem a bit creepy, just like film settings where people get murdered late at night. Not that anything like that would ever happen in St Aloysius's car park, I'm sure.'

Once we'd finally parked and walked back down to street level, I had my work cut out steering her to the nearest tram stop. Our original plan was to visit the apartment first, then look for the curtain material, but when I tried to hurry her along she said testily, 'Goodness, Sarah, what's the rush? There are all these sales on, and you might give a person half a minute to window-shop. Besides, it's too darn *hot* for scurrying, particularly when the city's as crowded as this with bargain hunters. Anyone would think that blessed flat will vanish into thin air before we can reach it!'

The most lavish sale in the world just couldn't be compared to inspecting the apartment, I thought, rescuing Aunt Dorothy from climbing aboard the wrong tram. The right one wafted us up the hill to the brink of the city and the apartment block. The only other time I'd seen it was when Dad had made a special detour while driving me back to school. It was caged in scaffolding then, and had just looked like any other half-built building. Even though it still wasn't completely finished yet, at last I was getting the chance to see inside! There were carpenters in the foyer, putting down a beautiful floor which Aunty Nat said was called parquetry. She stopped to chat to them, which was frustrating when I was so impatient to go on up to the apartment. And embarrassing, too, I thought, wishing she'd realise that it wasn't Ed Woodley and his mates, but *city* workmen. They probably wouldn't be used to gossipy old ladies asking their advice about the best way to put a shine on wooden floors. (Those patchy old floors at Avian Cottage weren't even remotely in the same league, anyhow.)

'The lift's *this* way, Aunty Nat,' I said, grabbing her

hand, but then it was Aunt Dorothy's turn to be embarrassing. She said she'd rather use the stairs.

'How do we know that thing's been properly tested if they're still doing work round the joint?' she demanded, but I certainly wasn't going to use ordinary stairs on such a notable occasion. I bundled both aunts into the lift and asked them to take a photo of me pressing the sixth-floor button. I got them to take another one while I was opening the door of the apartment with Piriel's key. Soon, very soon, I thought blissfully, I'd have a key of my own. Five weeks to the wedding, two weeks of boarding at school while they were away on their honeymoon, then – *this*. I'd just have a short tram trip home every afternoon, sail up in that smooth lift, then take my very own apartment key from my blazer pocket and let myself into the apartment . . .

The view was breathtaking, slamming itself at you through a wall of glass as soon as you set foot inside. On closer inspection, it wasn't really a wall, but large sliding doors leading on to a balcony. They opened as quietly as a whisper.

'You can see just about *everything*!' I cried. 'Oh, it's going to be so *spectacular* living here! Imagine what it must be like at night with the city all lit up!'

'I'm glad it's got a balcony,' Aunty Nat said. 'Only don't you go being a duffer, love, and falling over the rail. If you were any younger, I'd be worrying myself sick about that. It certainly is some view, though!'

'It's okay, but I think I prefer ones where you can

step right out into them,' Aunt Dorothy said. 'Like a nice big garden.'

'Isn't there supposed to be a garden around the back somewhere?' Aunty Nat said. 'It was on the plan Brett showed us, along with a swimming pool and sauna. Sarah might like to get photos of all that lot when we finish looking around inside. Better get rid of your cigarette first, Dorothy. It might be all right to puff away out here on the balcony, but I don't think you'd better inside the flat. Piriel mentioned she'd be making it a no-smoking zone for anyone coming to visit, and I'm pretty sure she meant *you*.'

'Oh well, I'll be quitting for good on New Year's Day,' Aunt Dorothy said virtuously, stepping back inside and managing to catch her thumb in the glass doors.

By the time I tugged her free, Aunty Nat had already found the kitchen and was opening and shutting everything like a little girl playing with a doll's house. I thought of the Avian Cottage kitchen with its ancient gas stove, and felt sorry for her. Piriel's kitchen had a range with six burners and a separate fan-forced wall oven. It also had a waste disposer, a retractable vegetable spray attached to the kitchen tap, and a foldaway ironing centre. Poor Aunty Nat, I guessed, must be comparing all that and feeling very discontented.

'Stone bench tops,' she said, awed. 'They're supposed to be a wonder for rolling out pastry.'

'Maybe Ed Woodley could copy the idea at your place. Piriel will know what it's called.'

'No need to ask her, dear. It's granite or marble or something. And though it looks the ant's pants in a modern place like this, I can't really see it at Avian Cottage. Dosho breaks quite enough crockery already.'

Marble had been used in the main bedroom ensuite, too, with its huge triangular spa bath set across one corner. That bath was so splendid I hoped I'd have one just like it, but the second bathroom was much smaller. There wasn't enough space for a tub at all, but to make up for that, it had an amazing circular shower cabinet made from glass bricks. Aunty Nat said it looked like something out of a science-fiction video, but I was so thrilled with it I got her to take a photo of me standing inside, even though there wasn't much room to aim the camera.

Then we inspected my future bedroom, which unfortunately didn't have much of a view. In fact, all you could see from that particular window was the concrete side of another building with a narrow alley full of parked cars down below. But it didn't really matter, because I'd be making the inside of that room so fabulous no one would even notice the lack of scenery. At the moment the walls were just bare plaster, but I imagined them painted a delicate sky-blue, as a background for the cloud curtain material. Horace's basket and my roll-top desk could go against the end wall. (That desk, even though it had once belonged to Aunt Dorothy and was covered with inkblots, biro doodles, cigarette burns and coffee-cup rings, was one item I'd hated to

137

put down on my discard list. I'd had it for so long I couldn't imagine doing my school assignments at anything else.) The cedar chest Aunty Nat had given me for my tenth birthday would have to be fitted in somehow, too. Not only would she be terribly hurt if I left it behind, but I'd have nowhere to keep all my odds and ends. Bed, bookcase of some kind, bedside table and chair – there might be problems working out just where to put everything in such a small space.

'If you've quite finished taking photos in here, Sarah, maybe I could get through to measure up for curtains,' Aunty Nat said. 'Then I think we'd better be moving along. There's still the pool and garden to see. You'll want to save some film for that before we go off hunting for the material you wanted.'

But it wasn't possible to photograph the pool or the garden, because there were more workmen around there pouring concrete. We couldn't get past, though Aunty Nat managed a quick look before they shut the security gate. 'It wasn't *all* a concrete jungle, you'll be glad to know,' she said as we went back to the tram stop. 'It's going to be very swish indeed. They've got a couple of gas barbecues and a bit of a lawn around the pool. There wasn't any water in that yet, which was probably just as well. Otherwise I might have been tempted to shin over that gate and have a nice cool skinny-dip, workmen or no workmen! Dosh, next time we come to visit, we must remember to bring our bathers.'

A fingernail slid in between my teeth before I could stop it. Somehow, the thought of the aunts using that pool jarred a little. The owners of all the other apartments would be like Dad and Piriel; professional, get-ahead, busy people, who would bring mobile phones down to the pool as well as towels. There had even been a photograph like that in the planning-stage brochure Dad had shown me. The idea of Aunt Dorothy in old navy bathers ploughing solidly along doing laps, or Aunty Nat frolicking about in her gross lace-pattern bathing cap, didn't fit in very well. There was no way in the world you could possibly mistake them for official residents. They just didn't look the part. They didn't even look as though they'd have relatives living in such a smart place.

'Next time we visit . . .' Aunty Nat repeated. 'Oh dear, I don't think I want to know about that! It's just hit me fair and square between the eyes . . . it's *you* we'll be visiting, Sarah, not just the other two. You'll actually be *living* here. It's going to be so hard to get used to, not having you around.'

'Well, I've only really been around at weekends and holidays,' I pointed out. 'The rest of the time I'm away at school.'

'Which is something I've *never* approved of,' Aunty Nat said frostily. 'You could just as easily have lived with *us* all this time, instead of being shunted around like a parcel when it wasn't even necessary. There are *oodles* of schools just as good as that one. Not that there's ever any arguing with that father of yours once he's made up his mind! The number of times I've just wanted to –'

'Well, I won't be boarding any more,' I said quickly, because although she hardly ever criticised Dad, it always made me feel troubled. I suspected that, deep down, Aunty Nat didn't really like him very much. There was the opal brooch he'd given her a couple of birthdays ago; although she loved opals, that particular brooch never seemed to get taken out of her jewellery box. And sometimes there'd be a coolness in her voice when she'd say, 'Your dad rang, Sarah. He's had to cancel this weekend, I'm afraid, but he'll try to take you out next Saturday instead.'

You'd have to be an awful kind of person to be in Aunty Nat's bad books, because she liked practically everyone. But Dad wasn't awful, I thought, suddenly feeling cross and muddled. He was *charming* to the aunts whenever he came to visit. The week Aunty Nat was in hospital having her varicose veins done, he'd sent the most enormous basket of flowers. He'd sent flowers to Mrs H. at the boarding house, too, once when I'd had to stay at school during a long holiday weekend. It was when the aunts were in New Zealand. The arrangements were that I'd be spending those four days with Dad, but unfortunately he'd been delayed in Perth, so it all fell through. Even though it must have been a pest for her, Mrs H. had been really nice to me. (Maybe it was because of the magnificent flowers.) *Everyone* thought he was charming – especially Eileen Holloway. That was because when he was visiting me at the aunts' one day, she happened to pop in, and he'd admired all the fairy greeting-card designs she insisted on showing him. (Eileen hadn't guessed he'd just taken his new contact lenses out to rest his eyes and couldn't see a thing up close.) Kids at school were impressed because he was so much better looking than their dads. The term I'd somehow managed to fluke top marks in maths, he'd given me a portable CD player to show how proud he was.

'No more boarding at school,' I said, turning my head for another look at the apartment block. 'The fortnight when they're away doesn't count, it will be over in a blink. After that, that's where I'll be – up there! It shouldn't take more than twenty minutes to get home every afternoon, so I'll be lazing around on the balcony before I do my homework. Then if it's one of Piriel's days when she gets home early, we'll be nicking down to the pool together.'

'I hope you'll be happy there, darling,' Aunty Nat said, giving me a little squeeze. 'You're a lucky girl, moving into such a posh place. My word, I'd better make sure I do a good job on the curtains when we track down that material!'

We had a long search for it, because scattiness seemed to run in the Gibbs family. (Mrs Gibbs's directions for finding the shop turned out to have as many mistakes as Belinda's homework.) But when we found it, they still had plenty of the cloud material left, and

Aunty Nat bought extra to make a matching doona cover. She wouldn't let me pay for it from my special holiday allowance, either.

'This can be a kind of New Year present from me,' she said. 'Your dad meant that holiday money for outings and such like, but you've hardly touched any of it yet. Why don't you go out somewhere with Corrie?'

'She's got her own friends,' I said. 'There's always kids popping in and out of their place. Or piling into the back of that rusty old four-wheel drive.'

'I'm sure Mrs Ryder wouldn't mind one more passenger when she drops them off to wherever they're going. Nor would Corrie.'

'They'd only be talking about their school and Parchment Hills stuff. I'd feel dumb, tagging along.'

'Well, maybe you'd like to invite some of your own schoolfriends out to Avian Cottage. If it's a long trip from where they live, they're more than welcome to stay the night.'

'I'd rather wait . . .' I began, but because it sounded rude to say I'd prefer to invite kids from school to the wonderful new apartment instead, I covered up with, 'It might be best to put that off until Ed Woodley finishes all the repairs. We'd only be getting in his way.'

Actually, there weren't any girls I *could* invite. Lots of people in my class got together in the holidays; I knew that from hearing them natter about various places they'd been to. Somehow, though, no one ever seemed to ask *me* along. All that would change, of course, when I moved into the apartment. Everything would automatically change for the better, because I'd be part of a real family group. Piriel's sparkle would rub off on me. I'd become so confident and popular . . .

'Oh look, there's a place that sells wedding-cake decorations,' Aunty Nat said when we finished at the material shop and went back into the arcade. Even though Piriel didn't particularly want one, Aunty Nat was determined to make a special cake. The best I could do now was to coax her out of buying a miniature bridal couple under an icing archway, and into choosing something plainer. While that battle was going on, we lost Aunt Dorothy. One minute she was there, elbowing marzipan wedding bells off the shop counter, then she just disappeared. We had a long search for her up and down the arcade.

'Holy mackerel!' Aunty Nat spluttered, sounding as though she really meant something much stronger. 'She *knows* we have to allow time for dropping the key off. Piriel made such a point about it. Darn that sister of mine! Sometimes, Sarah, I just wonder how Dosh ever manages to hold down a welding job in a factory! You'd think they'd be worried about her sticking all the wrong parts together.'

'There she is, coming out of that end shop,' I said, wondering why Aunty Nat seemed so jittery about the key being returned as soon as possible. It was almost as though she thought Piriel might be unpleasant if it wasn't.

'Of all the eccentric places to vanish into, Dosh – a *camping-gear* shop!' Aunty Nat scolded. 'We just about took this wretched arcade apart looking for you, but we never thought to check in *there*. You've never shown the slightest interest in tents, not even when you were in Girl Guides all those years ago! I seem to recall you kept wandering off and getting lost on hikes. And *that's* something that certainly hasn't changed.'

'I just went in there to get a Swiss army knife,' Aunt Dorothy said evasively.

'That's just as peculiar as tents! What on earth would you need one of those for?'

'It's not actually for *me*. It's . . . well, a little present for someone else. Theirs kind of got broken carving something.'

Aunty Nat still thought it was peculiar. She muttered all the way back to the St Aloysius car park, and kept it up on the drive to Piriel's office. Aunt Dorothy didn't defend herself or offer any more explanations. She just listened in a guilty pink-faced silence, opening and shutting all the Swiss army knife attachments.

Piriel was out, but as the receptionist expected her back soon, we were allowed to wait in her office. There were only two visitors' chairs, so I sat reverently at the gleaming desk, wishing Aunt Dorothy wouldn't slip off her shoes and massage her feet. (Maybe that was partly my fault for making her wear respectable shoes to town in honour of our apartment visit, but it looked peasant-like in such surroundings.) I glanced at the glossy folders on the desk, half pretending that I was Piriel and that I'd just clinched an impressive sale which had defeated everyone else in the firm. There was a grooved slab on the desk, holding three slender gold pens. Her name was on the door in gold writing. The chair I sat in was made of beautiful dark leather, with armrests. I could have sat there forever admiring all those wonderful things, but Aunty Nat began to look at her watch.

'We should be heading back to Parchment Hills now,' she said. 'I told Ed we'd be home before he left, to decide once and for all about the laundry floor tiles.'

'But I wanted Piriel to see the cloud material . . .'

'I know, dear, but if she's out showing someone over a property, there's no telling exactly when she'll be here. You'll catch up with her soon, anyway, because she'll be wanting to make a start on your dress for the wedding. We really can't hang around – Ed wanted to get cracking on those tiles first thing tomorrow. Just pop the key in the desk drawer, and we'll let the receptionist know on our way out.'

I slid open the top right-hand drawer. It contained only a box of tissues, a comb and mirror, and something wrapped in beige paper and raffia string. It was disappointing that Piriel hadn't had time yet to unwrap the paperknife I'd given her for Christmas, and put it out where everyone could see. I would have done it for her, finding a place of honour next to the exquisite gold pens, but somehow I didn't quite like to.

9

· · · · · · ·

New Year's resolutions

1. Practise eating restaurant food, like lobster and oysters. (Yuk!)

2. Find out how fax machines work (so I can help Dad and Piriel when they're busy).

3. Learn how to leave messages on answering machines without feeling stupid.

4. Somehow get a lot better at tennis.

5. Learn how to make interesting conversation with people.

6. Work really hard at that theatre workshop when I get there. (So Piriel won't think she's wasting her money.)

7. Try to get top marks for everything at school. (So

Dad won't think he's wasting *his* money.)

8. Stop biting my nails!

. . . .

I certainly wasn't next-door from *choice*. If I'd been given one, I would have stayed home and practised computer keyboard skills. (I wanted to be expert by the time Dad got back, so he wouldn't regret buying me such an expensive Christmas present.) But Aunty Nat and Mrs Ryder, gabbing as usual, had decided to go to an evening floral-art demonstration. It wasn't in Parchment Hills, so they wouldn't get back until late. The snag was that Aunt Dorothy had already taken off somewhere else on her own, and wasn't available as a minder. (Which was unusual, because she hardly *ever* went anywhere in the evenings. She'd announced that she was going to meet a friend, have dinner and then maybe see a film, but didn't give any more details.) Because Aunty Nat would never leave me at home by myself at night, I was bundled next-door with Mr Ryder and Corrie for company.

Corrie was down the street buying lemonade, so I had to sit in the living room for a little while making conversation with her dad. My voice felt stilted, but I tried my best. (Piriel didn't have any patience with people who claimed they never knew what to say. She said it was really just a lazy excuse for not bothering to learn adequate social skills.) So I made polite comments about the cricket, which he was watching on television, even though I didn't know anything much about it. (I can't say Mr Ryder had many social skills, either. He just sat there grunting at all my remarks and even turned the sound up quite loud at one stage.) I didn't think I'd ever be delighted to see Corrie Ryder, but it was certainly a relief when she came back with the lemonade.

'Dad always goes off into a coma when the cricket's on,' she said. 'Though it's pretty hard to tell the difference from how he is the rest of the time. The only way you can check up is by plonking an icy-cold bottle down on his bald spot. Like this . . .'

I glanced at Mr Ryder nervously, because my own dad wasn't a jokey kind of person, and I wouldn't have dared stir him like that, especially not in front of visitors. Corrie's one didn't seem to mind. He just told her he'd found a slab of cooking chocolate hidden away in the kitchen, and if she'd take half the blame when its rightful owner came back, he'd split it in two. Plus we could have some of his chips – but only if we both scrammed and left him in peace to watch the Windies get slaughtered.

Corrie put everything on a tray, saying we'd have a picnic in her room. It sounded very unhygienic to me, but when we got there, it was obvious that a few more stray crumbs on the floor wouldn't really make much difference. As well as crumbs and apple cores, there was a tree growing up out of the floor, reaching to the ceiling.

It wasn't a real tree, but *knitted*, with a crochet possum hanging from one branch. Corrie said it had taken two whole years to make, and the wool had come from worn-out sweaters collected from everyone in the street.

She seemed besotted with making things. The room was cluttered with glue bottles, paint brushes, stacks of paper, cardboard, matchboxes, cotton reels, bits of chicken wire, and lunch-wrap cylinders. The only chair was piled high with empty ice-cream containers. Corrie tipped them carelessly onto the floor so I could sit down, then dumped herself and the tray on the bed. The bedspread was made from denim patches sewn together, as though she'd also scrounged worn-out jeans from everyone in the street.

Imagining my own beautiful sky room at the apartment, I began to feel sorry for her. *Everything* in the room seemed to be recycled from something else. She didn't even have a proper bedside table, just a battered two-drawer filing cabinet. All her shoes, instead of being paired neatly in a special wardrobe rack like mine, were stored in a frayed wicker basket – maybe because the wardrobe was really a skinny metal gym locker. The strange thing was that Corrie didn't seem the least self-conscious about taking me into her room!

'Don't let me hold you up, if you want to be getting on with anything,' I said awkwardly. 'I could just as easily have stayed home by myself. It never gets dark till really late in summer, but Aunty Nat's always so clucky.'

'No worries,' Corrie said. 'I never plan what I'm

going to do after tea, anyhow. It's a case of whatever comes along – people dropping in, whatever's on the telly, or just mucking around. That's what I've been doing over at my Nan's place the last few days, mucking around. She got spooked when she read that newspaper thing about holiday crime figures. Her suburb was up near the top of the chart, so she asked me to go and stay while Pop was off on his fishing trip. It's okay over at her place, and we went into town and watched the New Year fireworks, but I was glad to get back home. Hey, while you're here, want to see what everyone gave me for Christmas?'

Most of her presents seemed to be stuff like T-shirts and gym shoes, the sort of ordinary, everyday things you'd just buy during the year when your old ones started to get shabby. None of them could compare with my computer, I thought, though Corrie seemed happy enough with them. She'd also been given a book about theatre costumes and make-up. It certainly wasn't the kind of present I would have liked, but she was pleased about it. She said it would come in handy for some puppets she wanted to make, and I almost told her about the theatre workshop Piriel had enrolled me in. But somehow, even just thinking about having to attend that workshop made my stomach feel like a coffee grinder. Besides, looking at Corrie's modest little paperback book, I thought it might seem like bragging to mention it.

'There, that's the lot, except for this wall-diary thing,' she said. 'I think it might be meant as a hint to get more with-it this year. I kind of let things happen.'

And that, I thought disapprovingly, was a very sloppy habit to get into. Dad had shown me how to draw up a chart for school, to make the most of my spare time in the evenings. (Though I'd learned to keep it out of sight, because Tara McCabe couldn't be trusted not to sabotage it. For instance, if I wrote down 'extra piano practice', she'd cross it out and scribble things like, 'Get a life!'.) But because I'd become used to following a worthwhile evening routine at school and not wasting time like Tara and everyone else, I automatically kept to one in the holidays, too. Tonight, for instance, if I hadn't had to come over to the Ryders', I might have got my stamp album up to date as well as practising computer keyboard skills. (That stamp collection was larger than anyone else's at school because of Dad having so many overseas contacts.) After doing all that, I could have played the game that had come with the computer. In spite of always feeling a bit guilty after what Piriel had said, it was a *fantastic* game. It was called *Rulers of Cedrona* and I was slowly working my way through level one. Next level up, I might have enough gold hoarded to train a more powerful army.

Corrie Ryder was inspecting the empty lemonade bottle as though *it* was made of gold. 'Just what I'm after for the bottom part of my lighthouse!' she crowed. 'I could paint it white and sprinkle sand on while it's still wet . . . Go ahead and have that last bit of chocolate,

Sarah. Mum's not likely to go mad at *you*, anyway; it's that cricket freak out there who'll get clobbered. He was the one who nicked it in the first place.'

'Thanks . . . that's if you're sure you don't want it,' I said, ashamed of looking greedy. I'd never eaten cooking chocolate before, except melted down in recipes, and thought it was delicious. 'What do you mean – lighthouse? How could you make one out of a lemonade bottle?'

'Easy. Pebbles stuck on a board might do for the base, though I haven't figured the sea out yet. Blue paint never really looks much like water. The top's one of those glass baby-food jars with a torch globe wired inside, so it can turn on and off.'

It seemed a lot of trouble to go to when you could *buy* miniature lighthouses. There'd been some in the toyshop where I'd gone Christmas shopping with Aunt Dorothy. Because I'd been thinking of a ship's-cabin theme for my apartment room round about then, I'd almost bought one to use as a decoration. They'd just been made out of painted wood, though, and didn't have lights that could be switched on and off.

'Maybe you could use real water and set the whole thing up in a cake tin or something,' I said, mildly interested.

'Now *that's* not such a bad idea! I don't think I'd better pinch any more stuff out of the kitchen cupboard; Mum's getting a bit fed up. But there's an old baking dish in the yard somewhere, from when I was making a plaster mould of my foot one time. Let's scoot down and get it.'

Corrie slid back the flywire screen and vanished through the window. I stuck my head out cautiously and saw that she'd run across the flat section of roof outside her room, and was climbing down a tree into their garden.

'I've got my good jeans on . . .' I called after her, but she either didn't hear, or didn't think it was important. I followed unwillingly, not being very keen on scrambling about in trees, or on carport roofs, either, no matter how flat they were. I stopped halfway across it, noticing all the improvements to our place next-door.

Aunt Dorothy had been toiling away outside just about every day since we'd moved in and the garden had lost some of its wild look. Parts of it were even quite impressive now. The summerhouse, repaired and freshly painted, sat on the terrace like a replica of the wedding cake Aunty Nat had made. In a few weeks' time, I thought happily, Piriel and Dad would be standing there for the marriage ceremony – that's if Aunty Nat didn't change her mind again and decide that the willow tree might be a more picturesque spot. She had half a dozen likely picturesque spots picked out. If it rained on the day, for instance, she planned to transform the living-room door into a kind of ornamental archway. (Eileen Holloway had already been organised to make a lot of paper rose garlands just in case.) But it couldn't possibly rain for Piriel's wedding! It had to be a perfect blue-and-gold day, just like this one had been.

The air today was so clear that you could decipher the tallest city buildings far away on the horizon. They looked magical, as though they were carved from blue glass. (Which wasn't the sort of thing you could have said to Ed Woodley. He claimed you could *always* tell where the city lay – you just had to hunt around for a layer of smog like thick brown gravy.)

'Hi, Piriel! It's *me* . . .' I whispered, imagining her somewhere over in that direction, amongst the blue glass buildings. Perhaps she might even have called in to inspect our apartment and was standing on its balcony at this very moment, somehow sensing my greeting. She'd gaze across the wide landscape in between and suddenly think, '*Sarah*. I could have sworn I heard her voice just now . . .' It *could* be happening like that. People who were emotionally close were supposed to be able to tune in to each other's thoughts and feelings. Telepathy, that was the correct name for it. The first time we ever met, Piriel had said that she knew we'd get along very well indeed. That *meant* she felt close to me – or at least I hoped it did.

Telepathy might work with the aunts, too. Once I'd actually moved into town, I could make a point of standing on that balcony every evening and sending a private message in *this* direction, to Avian Cottage. To Aunt Dosh, watering the garden late in the evening, murmuring to some plant, 'There, didn't I *say* your health would pick up if I moved you over to that corner?' Bumping her head on the hanging basket of ferns which she always

155

forgot about when she turned off the hose.

To Aunty Nat in the kitchen, humming along to one of her daggy tapes, wiping tears away with a floury potholder if it was a sentimental song, remembering a phone call she had to make and whisking into the hall to do it, forgetting about the phone call because she'd just noticed the linen cupboard could do with a good tidy.

Suddenly, the idea of sending secret messages to Avian Cottage wasn't warm and fuzzy any more. It was somehow *sad*, like the lost feeling that usually hit me after being dropped off at school by the aunts after a lengthy holiday break. Or even after an ordinary weekend. Mrs H. would be hovering around somewhere on the front steps to welcome everyone back. Tara McCabe said it was only to give a good impression and suck up to all the parents, but I was always grateful for Mrs H. being there on the steps. It meant a person to chat to about what I'd done over the break, an impersonal face to focus on, instead of having to watch the aunts' car disappear down the long, gravelled drive.

'Come on, Sarah, that tree's a cinch. It's safe as a ladder,' Corrie yelled.

I climbed unenthusiastically down into their yard. It was hard to keep up with her, because instead of keeping to the paths, she seemed to like plunging through shrubs and jumping over flowerbeds. I followed, wishing I hadn't made the suggestion about using real water for her ridiculous lighthouse.

'Could have sworn that old dish was lying around

here somewhere,' she said, hunting along the back fence. 'Or maybe it was down by the creek where I last saw it. That little creek's *fantastic*, isn't it?'

'I wouldn't know. I've never been to see it.'

'But it's on your own block of land! Crikey, fancy not going to have a look when –'

'It's Aunty Nat's block of land, not mine,' I said, slapping crossly at a mosquito. 'And it's going to get dark soon, so now's not the time to be charging off down there. Anyway, Piriel says they should sell that bush block. They've got quite enough garden to look after as it is, without any extra tacked on. It's only going to waste.'

'Dosh doesn't think it's a waste; she's *always* mooching around down by that little creek. There's a tree she likes to sit under and dangle her feet in the water. As soon as she finishes the top part of the garden, she wants to clear away all the dry stuff down there. I said I'd lend a hand.'

'She's probably only been sneaking off to have a smoke where Aunty Nat can't see,' I said even more grouchily, because I'd just found a slug on my good jeans. 'New Year's Day was when she gave up. At least that's what she claims, but she says it *every* year. She's been chewing gum instead whenever we watch TV lately, but that doesn't mean anything much. I just hope she won't be puffing away at the wedding, that's all. Piriel *hates* smoking.' (Though it wasn't slugs or mosquitoes making me annoyed. It was really Corrie

Ryder knowing things about Aunt Dorothy that I didn't, offering to help with gardening jobs. Anyone would think it was *her* aunt!)

'Would it be okay if I watched that wedding from our carport roof?' Corrie asked. 'I was going to invite a bunch of kids around so they could, too, but Mum said it might be pushing things, even if Aunty Nat doesn't have any objections.'

It wasn't even up to Aunty Nat, I thought indignantly, but suddenly remembered all the hours she'd spent preparing Avian Cottage for the wedding. If you wanted to chat to her these days, she had to be tracked down through a forest of recipe books. She was at it right up to bedtime, embroidering a new guest towel with wedding bells, polishing doorknobs, worrying about the finished cake. She kept moving it to different high shelves, so it would be safe from Aunt Dorothy.

'You could even chuck us up some party eats if you were feeling generous,' Corrie said cheekily. 'No one else needs to know.'

'Everyone will be eating inside,' I said in an off-putting voice. 'Aunty Nat's planned a kind of buffet meal, and I don't think I could be darting off outside with cakes and stuff. It would look really gross.'

'How about your *Little House on the Prairie* dress – did that turn out gross, too? Want me to arrange some kind of accident? It wouldn't be any problem. Spilled paint might do the trick. You could be showing me your dress the day before the wedding, and clumsy me could somehow –'

'Piriel hasn't actually started it yet, but she'll get around to it just as soon as she can,' I said coldly. (Maybe, I thought, that secret message I'd sent winging through the air like a sycamore seed might have planted itself in her mind. Right at this moment she could be thinking, 'I'll start Sarah's dress *tonight*. There's a possibility she might be feeling anxious about it. It has to be absolutely perfect, too; a very special dress for a very special person.')

'Anything Piriel makes is always marvellous,' I said, and headed back towards the house through the darkening garden. The Ryders' goat, straining against its long tether, bleated from the Avian Cottage side of the fence. There was a gap in the fence just there, so I kept my distance. That goat had a slobbering habit, I'd discovered, of pushing right up against you, as though you were its long-lost mother.

'Aren't you going to say hello to Meg?' Corrie asked, stopping to make a fuss over it. 'Only it's more like goodbye, because tomorrow she's going back to the farm where we borrowed her. They like other goats for company, so it's not fair to keep them cooped up by themselves for a long time. She just comes and stays with us every now and then.'

'The day we moved in, I thought she must be your sister or something,' I said. 'It was when you were handing those scones over the fence. You said you'd bring Meg over to eat our blackberries, only you never mentioned anything about a goat. It sounded more like a person.'

'Well, Dosh talks to her like she's a real person,' Corrie said, grinning. 'Meg doesn't even seem to mind cigarette smoke, either, though you'll be pleased to know Dosh *has* lasted a whole week since New Year. Ed Woodley's trying to quit, too. So they've been stashing what they would have spent on cigarettes in a jar, and whoever cracks first loses out. Aunty Nat's their banker. I reckon your aunts are *lovely*. It must feel awful, having to move into the city so far away from them.'

It was odd, I thought, how quickly darkness fell in mid-summer. Shadows, black as submarines, were gathering under all the trees, stealing across the lawn.

'They've been looking after you ever since you were a little girl, haven't they? Half your luck! My aunts are nice, too, but they don't treat me as anything special. They've all got their own families, so I'm just like one of the mob.'

'I'll still be coming out here to visit them.'

'Yes, but that wouldn't feel the same, would it? Though I guess you can hardly wait to move in with your dad, that's only natural. And Piriel, too, of course.'

A whole fleet of submarines, sly as thieves . . .

'Let's go inside,' I said abruptly. 'It's dark out here.'

10

· · · · · · · ·

Things I could do for the wedding

1. Horace – white ribbon bow. (Maybe better put it on while he's asleep, so he'll wake up and think it's *always* been there.)

2. Make a banner for front porch saying 'Congratulations Piriel and Brett – love from Sarah'.

3. Fill birdbath with little floating candles and flowers. (NB Scrub it out first!)

4. Disguise eagle ledge with trailing ivy.

5. Lock Aunt Dorothy's room so no one can go in there by mistake and see how messy it is, or make her tidy it up. (NB Hide all the ashtrays, too, just in case she gets tempted.)

6. Hide Aunty Nat's barnacle earrings.

7. Plus the bird wind chime Ed W. gave her for Christmas.

8. Sprinkle summerhouse floor with petals.

9. Put spare chairs in nice places all around the garden (eg fernery, under the willow tree, in the courtyard, over by the rose bed, so guests will appreciate all Aunt D.'s hard work).

10. Make Piriel and Dad feel very proud of me (eg try to sound brainy, and not bite nails in front of their friends).

. . . .

'You've . . . shifted in *already*?' I asked, clutching the phone a little more tightly.

'Yes, Sarah, at the weekend. They finished everything before schedule, and it seemed a waste staying on in that cramped place of mine with this one ready and waiting. Brett suggested it, actually, when he rang from New York. And it meant that all his stuff could come out of storage, with me here to keep an eye on it.'

'We've got some things of his, too,' I said dazedly. 'Things he didn't get around to packing, so Aunty Nat's minding them while he's away.'

'Yes, he mentioned that, which is partly why I've called – as well as wishing you Happy New Year, of course. Overdue, I know, but I haven't had a spare minute up till now. Would you happen to know if there's a chess set among those other items? Your darling dad's not sure if it went to Nat or the storage firm, so I'm just checking for him.'

'Yes, I remember seeing it,' I said. 'The pieces are made out of rock crystal, and the board's little squares of wood.'

Squares of silky wood, like a miniature version of the foyer floor at the apartment. I'd imagined that we'd all move into the apartment together, after they'd come back from their honeymoon. Together, we could have decided where everything should go. Dad would somehow find a miraculous way to fit all my things into my room . . .

'Oh good, I can tick off its whereabouts then. Brett said it was expensive, and we certainly wouldn't want to mislay it. Maybe one of you could drop it off some time, if you happen to be in town. It might look rather nice on the new coffee table I've just bought.'

I would have made them both coffee after we'd found places for all the furniture. When the last object was in place, we could have sat out on the balcony and watched the city lights, as a celebration.

'I've taken today off to get everything straight. There's still heaps to do, but with a bit of luck everything will be done by this evening. Brett's timing's very crafty – being away on the other side of the globe and not having to lift a finger. I just hope he appreciates all my hard labour when he comes back!'

Disappointments, I'd found, could be dealt with by concentrating very hard on nearby, everyday objects. I stared intently at the ornaments on Aunty Nat's phone table, as though seeing them for the first time. A jar of her jasmine hand cream, message pad, china pencil-holder (bought because of the seagulls painted on it), lace mat, bowl of daisies, one of Eileen Holloway's horrible pink ballerinas, a couple of loose wallpaper samples. It was also possible to wallpaper over your feelings, if you had to . . .

'Oh, I haven't asked if you're enjoying the holidays yet, have I, sweetie? How's the computer?'

'The girl from next-door is having a go on it right now,' I said. 'Corrie Ryder, her name is. They don't have one at their place. I don't mean I've *lent* it to her or anything; she's just using it downstairs in my room. She came over with a letter that wound up in their mail by mistake, and she kind of stayed. But she'd go back home again – if I had to go out somewhere . . .'

'I wouldn't let anyone else play around with that computer, Sarah. They're not the sort of thing you actually share. Anyway, must get off the phone now and slave on. The idiots put the couch in the wrong place, and you've got no *idea* how heavy it is to move. Bye, dear. Don't forget that chess set next time you visit . . .'

'Piriel, I could bring it in *right now* and help you arrange the furniture at the same time! I'm not really doing anything today. Can I?' I gabbled, but a heavy truck rumbled past Avian Cottage. I couldn't hear what she said, or even know if she'd heard me, because when the street was quiet again, she'd already hung up. I didn't ring back to check. It seemed stupid, when there wasn't any need. *Of course* she'd said yes!

I hurried downstairs to get ready, even though the aunts weren't available to drive me into town. Aunt Dosh had gone out with Ed Woodley to choose garden paving stones, and Aunty Nat to keep a hairdressing appointment. It was her six-monthly perm, so I knew she'd be there for hours. There was no way of knowing when Aunt Dosh would get back, either. She was probably driving Ed crazy right now, trying to decide between grey paving stones or brown ones. That could take hours, too. I'd just have to go by train.

'Was it your dad ringing from America?' Corrie asked. 'The way you charged up the stairs like that to answer, I thought you'd break your neck! Listen, I think I've finally worked out how to recruit more warriors! You could *trick* them into thinking you've got plenty of gold. What you do is . . .'

She was just as enthralled by *Rulers of Cedrona* as I was, even though she'd never played it before. Some of her tactics were wild, but she didn't seem to mind taking risks, even with the vicious ice-lady ruler in the next kingdom. I'd been sending that ice-lady grovelling messages and all my gold bullion so she'd zap other territories instead of mine. But Corrie, I noticed, was being more creative.

'It wasn't Dad after all. It was Piriel,' I said, getting

165

a clean shirt from my wardrobe. 'There's something she wants me to take into town for her, to the apartment. She's moved in early, so everything will be ready and the three of us won't have to bother about it after the wedding. Good idea, really. What time does the next train leave?'

'About twenty minutes. Aren't you going to wait until the aunts get home before you dash off?'

'They mightn't be back for ages,' I said. 'I'll just leave a note where they can find it. Piriel doesn't take many days off work, but she's got a free one today. I don't want to waste hours hanging around here. She's . . . *expecting* me, as soon as possible.'

That was undoubtedly what Piriel had said, only the truck had thundered past and blotted it out. She'd probably added that she'd be very grateful for my help. I changed my comfortable old sandals for a new pair I hadn't even worn yet.

'If the next train isn't an express, it's quicker to get off at South Moreton and catch the city bus,' Corrie said, switching off the computer. 'You probably don't know about that if you haven't travelled on the Parchment Hills line before.'

I looked up, confused.

'Otherwise the trip takes forever,' she added. 'You *sure* they won't mind you zipping off into town on your own? My mum's always a bit funny about it, unless there's a couple of us going in together. Aunty Nat might be even more –'

'If Aunty Nat was here to ask, she'd *let* me,' I said abruptly. 'It's not tearing off somewhere for the fun of it. I'm running a message for Piriel.'

'I could go in with you, if you like, so you don't get lost or anything.'

'Thanks all the same, but . . .'

'It's no trouble. I'd better ring Mum at the nursery first, but I don't suppose she'll put up too much of a fuss. Not if it's so important. She'd most likely get mad if I *didn't* go along with you.'

Saying that I preferred to go by myself sounded too much like a snub. While she made the phone call, I found Dad's chess set and wrapped it carefully in a double thickness of padding. I also slipped a scrap of the cloud material in my pocket to show Piriel. Corrie, permission given, ran next-door to make sure their house was properly locked up. I did the same at Avian Cottage, knowing Aunt Dosh could still get in because of the spare key kept hidden under the sundial. Then I waited at the Ryders' front gate, hoping Corrie would think to tidy herself up. Rumpled old shorts might be good enough for Parchment Hills, but they'd look completely out of place in that apartment block. Piriel might even think I *chose* to hang around with a thrown-together looking kid who did nothing but chatter!

Corrie, still wearing the shorts, chattered breathlessly all the way down to the station. Her hair looked like a bowl of tangled spaghetti, and I wondered if it would be too tactless to offer her my comb during the trip. I didn't get the chance. After we'd found seats, she went to say hello to some kids she knew up the far end of the carriage. While she talked to those other girls, she kept making little gestures at me, meaning that I should move up there and join them. But I pretended not to see and stayed where I was, hugging the chess set.

They were too much of a joke-sharing, things-in-common group, and I felt easier where I was. They gossiped together all the way to the next station. A crowd of other people got on there, and the seat beside me was taken. At the station after that, the carriage became even more crowded, and I lost sight of Corrie altogether until we reached the city and she squeezed out next to me.

'Sorry about that,' she said. 'But why didn't you come and sit with us while there was still room? You could have met Bron – she lives just round the corner from us. And Kelly and Tracey – they're in the same class as me at school. They were heading for the Moreton Centre, so they got off at South. I was a bit worried in case you didn't realise it was an express train and hopped off there, too. Remember how I was raving on about the bus connection? Just as well you stayed put, because I mightn't have been able to make a grab and haul you back in. There were just too many fat people and prams in between.'

'No one could miss all those City Express signs. I'm not *that* dumb.'

'Didn't say you were. It's just that going somewhere strange, people can make mistakes. Want me to take a turn lugging that parcel? It looks pretty heavy.'

'I'd better be responsible for it. It's a chess set, and the pieces are valuable because they're made out of crystal stuff. We've been minding it while Dad's overseas.'

'A chess set? What's so urgent about *that*?'

'Piriel wanted it back in a hurry because . . . because the security's better at the apartment,' I said defensively.

'Or maybe because she thinks crystal wouldn't last long in the same house as Dosh,' Corrie said. 'Are we catching a tram up to your place? Cool! I hardly ever get to ride on one!'

I wished she wasn't quite so keen about everything; it was embarrassing on the tram, sitting next to someone so energetic. When we reached the apartment block, she was even more of a pest. The glass entry doors weren't meant to have such a curious face and splayed fingers pasted up against them.

'Wow!' she cried. 'Just look at that floor in there – it's like a mirror! And one of those intercom things, too! Can I press the button to tell her we've got here? Only let's try some of the other ones first . . .'

'You mean the other apartments? What for?'

'Just for a laugh. We could freak people out by pretending we're van drivers delivering a grand piano. There's no way you could fit a piano in that little lift.'

'They'd probably be able to get it up the staircase.

And there's a service lift round the back somewhere, anyway.'

'Can't we go up in that, then? We could pretend *we* were a couple of grand pianos.'

'Stop mucking around,' I ordered, hastily buzzing our apartment before she could get at the intercom. 'Piriel? Hi, it's me. I've brought the chess set in . . .'

'*Sarah?* Good heavens, is Nat with you?'

'No, she was out when you rang, so I just . . .'

'Okay, you'd better come up, then,' Piriel said. 'I can't very well leave you standing around on the street, can I?'

She didn't sound particularly welcoming, I thought anxiously. Her voice had an edge to it, like teachers at school when people asked dopey questions about work which had already been covered in detail. I worried about it in the lift, just about biting Corrie's head off when she suggested hooning right up to the top floor and all the way down again. Perhaps I'd made a silly mistake and Piriel hadn't meant me to come in today *at all*. But although she looked startled to find two of us when she opened the door, she smiled nicely enough. When I introduced Corrie, I tried to drop a few hints that she wasn't really a *close* friend of mine. I knew Piriel wouldn't be impressed to think she was.

Corrie made herself at home straightaway, plunging out on to the balcony to gape at city landmarks. I followed, wanting to gaze at them again myself. But the balcony was sizzling with heat, and I was glad when

Piriel suggested almost immediately that we go back inside and see the rest of the apartment. (Corrie loudly cheering a passing fire truck might have had something to do with that.) Inside, now completed and furnished, looked fabulous! The living-room walls had been painted the palest shade of milky-beige, the same colour as the carpet, and the only ornament was a large earthenware pot filled with dried grasses. It seemed exactly *right*, just like the pair of beautiful smoke-coloured jars on the kitchen bench. Corrie started to fiddle with the stoppers on those jars, but Piriel quickly moved them out of reach.

'*Not* to touch my precious French vinegar and oil decanters!' she said. 'They're an early wedding present from a friend just back from Paris, and I treasure them very much indeed.'

The lamps in the main bedroom were treasures, too, she explained, showing them to us, but keeping a close eye on Corrie. The lamps were simple white spheres. I thought of my own bedside light, given to me by Aunty Nat years ago. It was bluebell-shaped, like something a fairy would wear on her head. Glancing at the elegant glass spheres, I knew I'd have to find some way of leaving that bluebell lamp behind at Avian Cottage when I moved. It just didn't belong here.

Corrie romped into the ensuite, exclaiming noisily at the triangular bath. I thought for one horrified moment that she was going to scramble right inside it with her grungy old gym shoes, but she was just leaning

171

over to inspect the spa fittings. There were cakes of soap piled in a bowl on the rim. Corrie, in her usual slapdash way, sent them toppling. I fished them all hurriedly out of the bath, because Piriel's eyebrows were starting to pleat. Everyone else except Corrie would have *realised* that such a perfect soap pyramid didn't happen by chance, I thought. It must have taken almost as long to create as the dried-grass arrangement in the living-room.

'You'd probably like to see Sarah's room,' Piriel said, herding Corrie firmly out into the hallway. 'Though I'm afraid it's rather a muddle, because I've had to use it to store a few bits and pieces. There was just *nowhere* else to put them. Still, we'll get everything straightened out sooner or later. Oh, and I hope you don't mind about the walls, Sarah. You were probably keen to do your own thing, but once the decorators actually started, it seemed better to stay with the one colour all through.'

Since I'd last seen it, my room had been painted the same creamy beige as the rest of the apartment. Which didn't matter in the least, I told myself quickly. Piriel was the expert when it came to interior decorating, and her choice must be the right one. Not that you could actually see a great deal of paintwork at the moment, anyway. The room was crammed with suitcases, an exercise bike, a home-gym treadmill, stereo equipment, a sewing machine, a swivel office-chair, and all Dad's computer stuff on a large work table just underneath the window. The new curtains framing the window were beige linen, the same colour as the walls.

Corrie Ryder, I remembered suddenly, had seen the curtain material I'd already bought. She'd come over one morning while Aunty Nat was cutting it out ready for sewing. (It was to ask me to the local pool with a bunch of her schoolmates, but I hadn't gone. In the first place, I didn't know any of those other kids, and secondly, Aunty Nat was likely to stick on a few ruffles if I wasn't there to stop her.) Before a certain person could open her big mouth, I said quickly to Piriel, 'I like those curtains you've put up. They're so nice and plain. Aunty Nat made some other ones, actually, but it was just cheap stuff we noticed at a sale. Nothing really special, and it's not as though they'll be going to waste. She can use them for Avian Cottage.'

'Oh, dear!' Piriel said. 'Now you've mentioned it, poppet, I *do* recall something about you choosing the curtains for this room. I completely forgot! All the dec-orating was done by the same firm, including the drapes, and I just didn't think . . . What a *shame* you'd already gone ahead and bought something else on your own.'

'Sarah's was blue with clouds on it. And there was going to be a special doona cover to match, too,' Corrie remarked, as though it was *her* business. If she'd known about the scrap of material in my pocket, I thought angrily, no doubt she would have insisted I drag it out to show.

'Well, a special doona cover probably won't even be needed for in here,' Piriel said. 'One of those couches that folds out might be more practical, because the room's so small. How about if we made it into something like an extra little sitting room? A converter couch would be handy if you happened to be staying at Parchment Hills and we had overnight guests. Then they could use *this* room – if you didn't mind, of course. What do you think, Sarah?'

For a moment I didn't really know *what* to think. It felt a bit like being back at school, with Tara McCabe saying, 'You're not spewing because I changed the beds around, are you? I wanted the one under the window. You weren't here to ask, so I just went ahead and moved all your stuff.'

'No, I don't mind,' I said slowly. 'I guess if we're short of space . . .'

'We can sort out the details after we've moved in and got ourselves into some kind of routine,' Piriel said. 'Right now, let's have a nice cold drink. I've got some absolutely delicious almond biscuits as well, though I'm afraid you'll have to be content with just two each. I'm expecting visitors later this afternoon.'

The biscuits were so thin you could almost see light filtering through each one, and they had come from a specialist bakery just down the street. When I lived here and asked people home after school, I thought, I'd stop at that same shop and buy yummy things for afternoon tea, too. Kids would be breaking their necks to get invited, once word had got around about my new lifestyle! Maybe I wouldn't ask Belinda or Tara, though. I couldn't quite see *them* appreciating delicate little almond wafers from a gourmet bakery. Jammy cream buns were more their style. They were almost as uncivilised as Corrie Ryder, who was dropping crumbs on the beautiful new coffee table. It had a polish on it like frost. Horace, I thought suddenly, would be rather a nightmare in the same room as that coffee table. He'd never managed to get it through his thick head that furniture legs weren't designed for sharpening claws. Aunty Nat didn't mind too much. She said her old furniture was so battered from Aunt Dorothy crashing into it, that a few extra scratches wouldn't matter. Piriel might not be so relaxed, though, about marks on her lovely glossy table . . .

'This room's nice, but the walls look a bit bare,' Corrie said, even though no one had asked her opinion. 'It needs pictures or a goldfish tank or something.'

'I *like* bare walls,' Piriel said, obviously finding her a bit hard to take. 'And I've never really understood why people want to load themselves with pets. I've never felt the urge to acquire one myself. They're such a nuisance if you want to go away anywhere.'

'You can get automatic timers for fish food,' Corrie persisted.

I wished she'd shut up about fish tanks. It reminded me of a quarrel between Aunty Nat and Dad a couple of years ago, and even though it had just been angry words over the telephone, I still hated thinking about it. Aunty Nat hadn't realised I was sitting outside and could hear every one of those sharp words through the open window. I'd been waiting for Dad to come and pick me up. We were going to buy an aquarium for my birthday; a proper tropical one, not just a little tank with a couple of goldfish. He'd said we'd do a whole lot of other things before that, spending the whole day together as a birthday treat. Stuff like a boat ride up the river, feeding the ducks on the lake in the public gardens, visiting the dinosaur exhibition, and I was looking forward to all that *much* more than being given an aquarium. (Tropical fish always made me think of dentists' waiting rooms, but I hadn't liked to say so when Dad had already suggested it as a present.)

He was late, so I was threading periwinkle flowers into a chain to make the time go faster. (Blue periwinkle was really a weed – I looked it up in one of Aunt Dorothy's gardening books. Its correct title was *Vinca major*.) The phone had rung in the living room, Aunty Nat answered it, and suddenly her voice began to sound like a wasp trapped against glass. (It was actually almost impossible to make a chain out of *Vinca major*; the stems were too fragile.) Aunty Nat was saying furious things to Dad; that she was sick of being the one to break the news about cancelled outings; how selfish he was; that he didn't *deserve* to have a child; how no one would even *guess* he was a parent, for all the interest he took. (Making proper slits in flower

stems with bitten-down nails was difficult.) Aunty
Nat's voice was like a whole swarm of angry wasps. She
dragged boarding school into it, saying I'd just been
dumped there because of out-of-sight, out-of-mind
convenience; that anyone whose conscience was eased
by a whole lot of ridiculous expensive presents should
feel ashamed of themselves, that anyone so conceited
and arrogant –

She slammed the phone down after saying all those
things. I'd thrown the useless flower chain away and
crept around the back quietly so she wouldn't know I'd
overheard. It wasn't even *true*, anyhow; Aunty Nat had
got it all wrong. When I moved to the apartment, she'd
see just how wrong she'd been. Dad, Piriel and I would
have a *fantastic* time together. We'd take boat rides up
the river, feed the ducks in the gardens, go to museum
exhibitions. Every weekend we'd be doing something
different, and not only weekends, either, but every
afternoon. There'd be all that free time after school . . .

'Looking forward to the theatre workshop starting,
Sarah?' Piriel asked.

I immediately found myself wishing Corrie *would* go
on boring everyone about fish. I still didn't like to be
reminded of that workshop. If Piriel knew someone
who taught there, they might report back to her how
hopeless I was!

'Theatre workshop?' Corrie said inquisitively. 'Is that
like acting lessons? You never told me you were . . .'

'It was a Christmas present. It's going to be terrific

and I can hardly wait,' I lied, then hurriedly changed the subject. 'I've been getting my school things ready, Piriel. That'll be one job out of the way before the wedding. It felt funny, though, not having to bother about the boarding-house list this year. Just a little suitcase to see me through the first couple of weeks, then I'll be able to –'

'Actually, Sarah, there might be occasions when you'll still have to board,' Piriel said. 'Technically you'll be a day-girl from now on, of course, but there'll be times your father and I both happen to be away. You couldn't very well stay here by yourself then, could you? Such as after Easter when Brett's off to Tokyo for three weeks and I might go along for the trip. There'll be other times, too, when we'd both have to go straight from work to various things and not get home till all hours.'

'That part should be okay,' I said eagerly, wanting her to know how self-reliant I could be. 'I wouldn't get nervous here on my own, not with the security cameras and the intercom and everything. Even if you were both going to be late back . . .'

'Well, we'll see. Brett *did* say he'd come to some arrangement with the school for the odd weeknights, so it's up to him. And if we're ever away for weekends, I guess you could always go to Nat's as usual . . . How are the renovations coming along, by the way?'

'You should see it!' Corrie said. 'Ed's painting the out-side now, white with green trim round the windows. And their little summerhouse is the same. Mum's hoping Dad will get shamed into doing something about *our* place.'

'Aunt Dorothy's planted roses all around the summerhouse. They've got masses of flowers on them, so you'd be able to use it for wedding photos,' I said. 'And we've bought a new sun-umbrella for the deck table. It's green with a white fringe, but Aunty Nat won't put it up yet. She wants to save it for the wedding.'

'I really wish the old dears wouldn't carry on as though Avian Cottage is an established fact for the wedding,' Piriel said abruptly. 'You, too, Sarah. You're starting to sound just like them, you know.'

'But I thought you'd –'

'It was only an *option*, nothing more. I haven't decided yet. Another possibility was having it in Sydney, which is what we originally planned. Brett has work to do there when he gets back from the States, and I've got heaps of people up there I want to catch up with, too. It would certainly save a lot of travelling back and forth if we based ourselves there for a few days. Goodness, neither of us wanted all this great fuss made about the wedding! I really *wish* Nat would wait until I give her the green light to go ahead. She's just taking it for granted. And if there *is* a last-minute change of plans, it's going to mean hurt feelings for her, and awkwardness for *me*.'

'She'll probably feel a bit disappointed,' Corrie said.

I looked at her quickly to see if she was being sarcastic, because I knew that disappointment wasn't the right word at all. Aunty Nat would be devastated.

'There's no denying that Avian Cottage is the most

179

attractive old place,' Piriel went on. 'Or at least it will be when what's-his-name finishes the repairs. I quite *like* the idea of having it there, and it was sweet of Nat to offer. But she seems bent on turning the whole thing into such a ghastly, over-the-top affair. All Brett and I want are just a few friends around for drinks, after the registry-office part is out of the way. Either here, or in Sydney, it doesn't really matter which. Even the friends and drinks bit isn't all that vital.'

But . . . Aunty Nat's already made the cake, I thought helplessly. She's spent hours piping little icing designs on a board every night, getting her hand in for the real thing. Her wedding bells guest towel has just had satin bows sewn on the corners. She's polished all the brass doorhandles so you can see your reflection in them . . .

'Goodness, look at the time!' Piriel said. 'Sorry, but I'll have to throw you two out now. My visitors will be on the doorstep soon, and I want to have a shower before they get here. Pity I didn't know you were coming, Sarah, otherwise I might have been able to put them off. We'll be talking business, so you'd be very bored if you stayed. Actually, it might be a sensible idea next time to let me know if you plan to drop in. Just in case I've made other plans.'

'I'm sorry,' I mumbled, turning bright red and avoiding Corrie's eye. 'There was a truck going by while we were on the phone. I really thought you said to –'

'I didn't mean you had to charge all the way into town with that chess set, specially in such a heatwave. Still, now it's here, we might as well see how it looks on display . . . Oh, for heaven's sake, child, be *careful*!'

Corrie, jumping up helpfully to get the chess set from where I'd left it on a chair, had fumbled and dropped it. There was a moment of tense silence. It would be awful, I thought, if Piriel scolded her. Somehow you just couldn't tear strips off someone so well-meaning and cheerful, no matter how aggravating they were. But Piriel, I remembered, *could* tick people off quite bluntly. I'd heard her do that once, when we'd gone to collect her car from being serviced and they hadn't fixed something she'd specially pointed out. Although she hadn't raised her voice, listening to it had been . . . chilling. Piriel, I thought, having such high standards of efficiency herself, must find it maddening when other people fell short. I was glad I hadn't fallen short yet.

Luckily, nothing was damaged. Corrie, whose face had crumpled with alarm for once, let out her breath in a great whoop of relief. The chess set, arranged at one end of the coffee table, looked as though this particular room had been designed on purpose to hold it. Piriel was very pleased with the effect, and came right down into the foyer to see us off.

'Next time we'll make it a proper visit, Sarah, so you can use the pool,' she promised. 'It's been filled with water now, you'll be glad to hear. Better not go

181

around to have a look, though; save it for another day. These traffic lights always take ages to change, so you'd better nip across to the tram stop while the going's good. Bye for now . . .'

I glanced back while we waited for the tram, but she'd already gone back inside the apartment block. In a few weeks' time, I thought, I'd be there with her to help entertain visitors. I'd make it one of my jobs to buy things like almond wafer biscuits on the way home from school. Piriel would be pleased by the organised way I made lists, so that nothing important was ever overlooked or forgotten . . .

'Your dad's girlfriend sure is pretty!' Corrie said, which made me thaw a little towards her. I even thought of saying I'd do my best to get her invited properly to the wedding. But then, spoiling all her chances, that ignorant, opinionated, foot-in-the-mouth Corrie Ryder added, 'I'm glad it's you and not me that's got to live with her, though! I reckon she's just like –'

'Like *what*?' I demanded.

'Like the ice-lady ruler in the next kingdom. And she never even thanked you for bringing in that stupid-looking chess set, either!'

11

. . . .

Improvements to Avian Cottage

1. Floors flat. (Well, *flatter*, anyhow.)

2. Doors fixed.

3. Wiring checked.

4. New plumbing in downstairs bathroom.

5. Even the pelican tiles don't look too bad in there now the walls are painted. (NB Train Aunt Dosh not to leave her gumboots lying around in nice new downstairs bathroom.)

6. Leaky roof mended.

7. Eagle shelf buffed up with tan boot polish, missing eye replaced with yellow bead from one of Aunty Nat's old brooches – looks okay now.

8. New house number on gate. (Eileen didn't do such a bad job with the flying swallows after all.)

9. Whole garden tidied up.

10. Avian Cottage painted inside and out. Looks quite nice, really (ie looks *terrific*).

• • • •

My Cedrona knights lolled inside the fortress and just sent out warrior apprentices who weren't really much practical use. The ice-lady, having sized up the situation, was threatening total invasion, and I didn't have any more gold to use for bribes. My border bristled with menacing triangular flags, like shark fins. It was hard to concentrate on the game, anyhow, because of Ed Woodley's clattery trips through the courtyard. This was his last day at Avian Cottage, and he was packing up all his gear. No more tripping over paint-roller trays in the hallway, I thought; no more dodging ladders or being sent down the street to buy peculiar things like tap washers, wing nuts, grouting, or a new caulking gun (the other one broke when Aunt Dorothy dropped it off the roof while helping him seal a gap round the chimney). It would feel strange not having Ed around. I'd even got used to his corny jokes at morning tea, lunchbreaks, afternoon tea and all the times when Aunty Nat had invited him to stay for dinner.

I froze the game, leaving the computer switched on

in case any last-ditch solutions came to mind. On the other side of the cloud curtains, Ed Woodley strode by with a load of planks balanced across his shoulder. Aunty Nat had been quite pleased that those curtains weren't needed at the apartment after all. Although she'd had to add a flounce to make them long enough to fit this window, it didn't matter much because she'd already sneaked a frilly edging onto the new doona cover. In spite of that, they looked nice against the freshly painted walls, which were pale-blue, except for the one covered with the big forest poster. I'd got used to looking at it first thing in the morning, so I'd asked Ed to leave it as it was. People staying here overnight when this room became the guest room might like it, too. I glanced around at the items I'd have to leave behind, wondering if those guests would think they were awful. Perhaps not. Avian Cottage was full of old stuff that didn't match properly, so even the shabby roll-top desk I'd inherited from Aunt Dosh just blended in somehow. So did my cedar chest. Maybe I'd be able to reclaim both of them one day, if Piriel and Dad found other places in the apartment for their exercise bike and home-gym treadmill. It was going to be *traumatic*, not having that roll-top desk to do homework on.

Someone banged on the courtyard door. I could see Corrie through the stained-glass magpie panel, but because of the remarks she'd made about Piriel, I didn't smile at her when I opened the door.

'No one heard me knocking upstairs, so that's why

I came round the side,' she said, irritatingly snub-proof. 'Dad sent over these plants for your little courtyard. It's just a few handfuls, but it spreads like crazy if you keep it damp. We could dig it in now, if you like.'

The plants were wrapped in damp newspaper, and she wasn't even bothered about the muddy water trickling down the front of her shirt. If it was meant as a gift, then it was a *ridiculous* one to give a person who'd soon be moving to a different place.

'Thanks,' I said coolly. 'But I'm busy with something else right now. If you dump that down somewhere, I'll let Aunt Dorothy know. I think gardening's more of a hobby for *elderly* people.'

Corrie still wasn't put off. She just raved on about various loopy ideas she'd had for the Ryders' own garden. (One of them was growing a huge maze down the back and charging admission, and another was learning about topiary so she'd have a whole yard full of tree-animals.) 'You could do interesting things like that in your courtyard,' she said. 'On a smaller scale, of course, but there's still enough room. There's an old statue in our shed if you want it. It's a lady in a nightie thing holding a flat bowl, and the bowl's meant to be a bird-bath. All it needs is —'

'That's the very *last* thing I'd want. The birds round here certainly don't need any encouragement. They already squawk around the house all day long. Specially those grey ones with the spotty bands around their necks.'

' "Janine just flew! The sky is blue!" '

I stared at her, eyebrows raised.

'Don't mind me,' Corrie said. 'It's just that funny call doves have, like saying a phrase over and over. It sounds as though they're on the phone gossiping to each other all the time. "It's up to you! I burned the stew!" Listen, there's one at it right now . . .'

Far down in the garden I heard a dove call quite distinctly, 'Have *you* seen Hugh?', repeating it several times like a recorded message. 'He just shot through,' another one answered obligingly. I'd always thought the noise those doves made for hours on end was monotonous, but I suspected that from now on they'd be totally infuriating! Just as maddening as Corrie, who noticed the computer screen was on and darted inside before I could do anything about it. She didn't even wipe her shoes on the mat. (That mat's days were numbered. Aunty Nat had ordered a new folk-art one from Eileen Holloway, with magpies on it to match the door.)

'You've certainly landed in *big* trouble!' Corrie said, after switching to 'play' without even asking.

I inspected the ice-lady's pennants gloomily. All the poor little apprentice knights had taken fright and were scurrying back towards the castle.

'Trying to make those lazy big-shot fighters come out is a pain in the neck,' Corrie said. 'It wastes too many points. There's no use trying to smarm up to *her*, either. It only works for a little while, and she just wants more and more in the long run. Maybe we could try something else. How about building an extra fortress way over the other side? With a bit of luck she mightn't notice . . .'

She began to make a secret road across the marsh, heading towards the snowcapped mountains of Cedrona. The ice-lady soon twigged to what was going on, and seething with outrage, dispatched twenty of her fiercest knights. Our road builders downed their tools and ran. A few minutes later, an alien banner shot triumphantly up on our castle tower and the game was over.

I switched off the computer and started to brush my school blazer. It didn't actually need brushing, having been drycleaned only last week. The name-tag was loose, though, so I found some grey cotton and sewed it back into place. Everything I wore at school had a name-tag, because of living at the boarding house. Corrie probably never had to worry about labelling all *her* clothes, I thought, looking at the blazer, the neatly rolled grey socks, the five gingham dresses with white collars, feeling suddenly depressed. I didn't even *like* that uniform. Or the school, either.

Corrie tried my prissy hat on in front of the mirror. 'Just as well *I* don't have to go there,' she grinned. 'This thing makes me look like one of those dopey Cedrona knights. You know, it's weird, Sarah, how you never seem to talk much about your school. The other kids or anything . . .'

'It's a *terrific* school,' I said huffily. 'We're getting a new Physical Education and Sports Complex this year.

It's *enormous*. I can hardly wait to get back and see all my friends again. Specially Tara. She's so funny, she always has everyone in fits. She started boarding the same year as me, and we always kind of end up sharing the same room . . .'

Though that wouldn't happen this year, I thought, because of not being a proper boarder any more. I'd just be staying there occasionally when Dad and Piriel were away. That would most likely mean sleeping in the tiny single room next to the shower and toilet block. No one could get much sleep if they were put in there, so normally it was just used to store luggage. But sometimes it doubled as temporary accommodation. Besides, Tara had already asked Mrs H. if she could move in with someone else this term. Ages ago, before I'd even known I'd be a day-girl this year, she'd asked Mrs H.

I put all my school things back into the wardrobe. There was a photo album on one of the shelves, a beautiful gold-embossed expanding one Dad had bought for me in Rome. There was also a box of loose photographs which needed sorting out. Arranging items in order seemed an ideal job at that moment, somehow comforting. I tipped the box contents onto the bed.

'Is this your father?' Corrie asked, glancing through the album. 'It must be like having a movie star for a dad!'

It *was* a nice photo. Aunty Nat had taken it at the airport, the first time he'd gone to the UK. Dad didn't usually like to be seen off on trips, but because he was going to be away for so long, he'd made an exception for that one. Corrie turned a page to an even better photograph of him, taken when he'd married Lorraine. They *both* looked like movie stars, posed underneath the canopy of some London hotel, smiling at the camera. It always felt peculiar coming across that picture, though. Unreal, somehow, like looking at faces in a magazine. I sometimes even felt that Lorraine mightn't have existed, except in my imagination. There were just those few letters she'd written, memories of being wild with excitement, memories of telling everyone at school that I wouldn't be boarding next term, that I'd be living in a house with my dad and new stepmother. Then, nothing.

'Who's that with him?' Corrie asked. 'Piriel, isn't it?'

'*Piriel*? Of course not! That's just someone Dad met when he was working in London once,' I said briefly. 'They got married, but it didn't work out. So then they got divorced.'

'Oh . . . sorry,' Corrie said, but added, 'She really *does* look like Piriel, though. They've both got the same kind of eyes and expressions and everything.'

I didn't say anything, writing dates and captions on the backs of all the recent photos I'd taken. Sometimes pictures could slip out of album pages, so it made sense to label each one neatly beforehand. Keeping *everything* in order was important. It was like having a map, a compass.

'They even kind of *dress* the same,' Corrie claimed, examining the photo of Piriel I'd shown around at school. 'You know, everything all smooth and silky.'

'They've both got important jobs, so *naturally* they've got to look smart all the time,' I said, taking the album from her and slamming it shut. 'It's rubbish, anyhow, saying they look like each other. Anyone can see they're not. It's just as dumb as that thing you said the day we went into town, about Piriel being like the ice-lady.'

'Oh, that . . .'

'Yes, *that.*'

'I didn't mean anything, really. It was just something that slipped out.'

'Were you by any chance hinting that Piriel's kind of bossy?'

'Well . . .'

'People *could* get that impression meeting her for the first time, but they'd be way off the mark. She might sound a *little* bit bossy every now and then, but –'

'Sarah, honestly, I never . . . Oh damn, Mum says I'm always blurting out things without thinking first! Dad reckons you can't take me anywhere.'

'It's just that she's got very high standards about everything, and I certainly don't see there's anything wrong with *that*. It was a rotten thing to say. That ice-lady's so nasty, sneaking around trying to get her own way all the time and not caring about anyone else. Piriel doesn't even *look* anything like her! That ice-lady's got pale-blonde hair down to her waist, and Piriel's happens to be dark red, in case you haven't noticed. So *there!*'

I was starting to sound a bit like Aunty Nat and

Aunt Dorothy in one of their squabbles. Or worse still, like Jessica and Jasmine Werner in the school boarding house. They were always running off to snitch on each other to Mrs H. Once Jessica dragged her mattress into the corridor, saying she'd rather sleep out there than share the same room as her pig of a sister. (That was because Jasmine was cutting her toenails and a clipping shot across the room and landed in Jessica's ear.) In a minute, I thought, *I'd* be threatening to go next-door and tell Mrs Ryder on Corrie.

'I'd better get on with all the other things I have to do,' I said less fiercely, finding to my surprise that I didn't particularly *want* to quarrel with Corrie Ryder. She wasn't so bad, really. In fact, I kind of *liked* her. 'There's a phone call I have to make. Dad got back from overseas last night – well, not back exactly, because he has to stay over in Sydney for a few days. He called Aunty Nat from the airport to let her know. I was asleep, but he said if I ring round about now there'll be time for a chat.'

There was a lot I wanted to talk to him about. School, for instance. And if something could be fixed so that I wouldn't have to board there any more, even temporarily. If he could somehow find out if Piriel had been able to make my dress for the wedding, because I felt so awkward about asking her personally. How nice Avian Cottage looked now; how excited Aunty Nat was about holding the wedding there; that she'd be so devastated if it didn't happen . . .

'I'll nick off, then, and leave you to it,' Corrie said,

getting up. 'Oh . . . and Mum wanted to know how many extra glasses Aunty Nat needs. You know, wine glasses for the wedding – Mum was helping her out with them or something.'

'Aunty Nat's down at the supermarket, but I'll tell her when she gets back.'

'No worries. And Sarah . . . I'm sorry about that other stuff. You'll have a *great* time when you move to the city. See ya!'

'Come over tonight and we'll have another go at *Rulers of Cedrona*,' I said impulsively. It was only after she'd nodded and run up the path to the front gate that I realised it was the first time I'd ever actually invited her. All the other times, I'd just left it to *her* to show up, and hadn't exactly been very welcoming when she had. Feeling ashamed, I went upstairs to phone Dad, first checking my watch to make sure it was ten-thirty precisely. (He'd told Aunty Nat that it wasn't any use ringing before then, because he'd have business to attend to.) The receptionist put me through and we talked for a few minutes, although Dad did most of it. (He told me all about his trip, trying to fit it in quickly, as he had a meeting scheduled for the rest of the morning.)

'Sorry – hang on a minute,' I broke in. 'Horace just got tangled up in the phone cord.'

'Still the same old Horace, eh?'

'He's *beautiful*; I wouldn't swap him for any other cat in the world! I'm getting him a new tag with the apartment address for his collar. You don't think there's any danger he'll fall in the swimming pool when we move there, do you? Cats are supposed to be able to swim, but Horace mightn't . . .'

'Perhaps now's the right time to mention this, Sarah,' Dad said. 'You'll have to know sooner or later. The thing is, pets just aren't allowed in those apartments. The regulations are very strict about it, but you're such a sensible girl I know you won't have any trouble accepting what can't be helped. I meant to break the news before I left, but Aunty Nat said to wait. She didn't want to spoil the school holidays for you, I guess. Piriel was planning to drop a hint if she got the chance, but she wasn't too keen about being in the hot seat. I hope it's not too much of a blow. It's not as though the cat's got to be put down or anything like that, and I'm sure Nat won't mind giving it a permanent home at Avian Cottage.'

Well, I told myself briskly, that solved the hassles of litter-tray training when Horace thought it was so undignified. It took care of a whole stack of problems, really – worrying that he might fall off the apartment balcony, cough fur balls on the expensive new carpeting, knock over those sphere lamps, tumble into the pool, the trauma of another move. Horace was used to being with the aunts, anyway, and seeing me just on weekends and in term holidays.

'It's . . . okay,' I said, hoping my voice didn't sound quavery. 'I should have realised there might be some rule like that. It's probably for the best. Horace just got settled in at Avian Cottage, so it wouldn't have been fair to shift him again.'

'Good girl,' Dad said approvingly. 'I didn't know what I was going to do if you went hysterical on me. Tell you what, we'll buy something or other to make up for it. How about your own personal television for the apartment? Then it wouldn't matter if we're watching a program that clashes with one of *your* favourites. Now, another important thing . . . Would you let Aunty Nat know that we've decided to get married in Sydney? I didn't mention anything to her last night when I rang, because the details weren't finalised then.'

'*Sydney?* But she's . . .'

'Concentrate, sweetheart, so you can pass the message on properly. It will be next Wednesday, two o'clock, and we've ditched the reception idea. We're just heading for the airport straight afterwards. But if you'd like to come up for the registry-office business, we could fly you up, that's no problem. Arrange something with Piriel. I'm meeting her for lunch back at our hotel when I finish here, so I could get her to give you a buzz.'

I hadn't even known Piriel had gone to meet him in Sydney. She hadn't phoned to let me know, or to say goodbye or anything.

'I hear the old girls wanted to have some kind of shindig out at their place, so it's just as well Aunty Nat happens to be out shopping right now, isn't it?' Dad said. 'I could have got my ears boxed over the phone, otherwise. Piriel said it was all pretty heavy going, and

195

she didn't quite know *what* to do when they suggested it.'

'But at Christmas she seemed –'

'Listen, smooth down any ruffled feathers if necessary, there's a darling. What we could do, I suppose, is fly the *three* of you up here next Wednesday. We wouldn't have time to take you around sightseeing, before or after the wedding, but you could go out on the town by yourselves. How would that be as a cure for ruffled feathers?'

'They don't like planes,' I said slowly. 'Aunt Dosh gets airsick, and Aunty Nat always thinks the pilot might die of a heart attack. It was in some old film she saw and one of the passengers had to crash-land. Even when they went to New Zealand that time, they got there on a cruise ship.'

'Well, not to turn it into a big issue, Sarah, there's a good girl. We'll sort something out. But not to fret, either, if you don't make it to the registry office. As I explained before, you'd be the only ones there except for us. Marriage is really just something between the two people concerned. Besides, we'll be seeing you when we get back in a few weeks, won't we? Look, I've got to go now, can't very well keep a whole marketing team waiting . . .'

I replaced the phone and went back downstairs and out into the courtyard, tripping over Corrie's bundle of plants. Even though I didn't like getting my hands dirty, I decided to plant them safely, before the afternoon sun crept around to that side of the house. It was something to do, anyhow, a distraction, seeing I'd run out of odd jobs inside. The plants were a bright, clear green, as though they'd been laundered, with little tear-shaped leaves. Plants needed cosseting after being put in; I knew that from watching Aunt Dosh. She always used the watering can, because she said it was gentler than a hose. I went around the back to find it, ducking under the fronds of the willow tree. Piriel said it should be chopped down, because willow roots damaged drains. I hadn't known that, but it must be true if Piriel said so. It seemed a shame, because that big tree was glorious, like an illustration from an old-fashioned fairytale book. Still, that wasn't my concern; if it had to be chopped down, I wouldn't even be here to notice the loss.

The watering can was kept in the fernery, underneath the overhead decking. When we'd moved in, that fernery had been an eyesore, just something you hurried through as quickly as possible to reach the terrace. Aunt Dorothy had done wonders to it. She'd cleared away all the weeds from the poor choked ferns, then hung trailing plants in baskets from the deck slats, things that liked shade. It looked lovely now, like a cave full of green stalactites. Dad had never had much patience with Aunt Dosh; she bored him. He didn't think she was interesting in any way, or had any views that were worth listening to. He hadn't let me visit her when she lived in the caravan park, before she moved in with Aunty Nat. Only losers ended up in caravan parks; he'd said so.

The watering can wasn't on its slab, under the tap. I stood amongst the ferns, my thoughts ticking along vaguely. The doves were calling to each other again down in the garden. I listened carefully, but it seemed to me that the messages weren't cheerful little gossipy messages at all; they sounded *mournful*. Phrases like, 'They don't want you. You're last in the queue. Just room for two . . .'

Perhaps the watering can was down in the summer-house, I thought, weaving back through the willow fronds. Aunt Dosh might have used it for the roses she'd planted around the base of the summerhouse specially for the wedding. She needn't have bothered, really. It was going to take place thousands of kilo-metres away now, with no ceremony or anything, no celebration. Dad and Piriel would be leaving straight afterwards to catch a plane to wherever they were going for their honeymoon. Dad didn't seem to mind about there being no guests or ceremony of any kind; he'd even left it up to me to decide if *I* wanted to be there or not. He'd said on the phone, 'Marriage is really just something between the two people concerned.' Maybe he was right; he was usually right about things, just like Piriel. But when *I* got married, I thought sud-denly, I'd want the aunts around. It would be *heartbreaking* if they weren't at my wedding; Aunty Nat, dabbing at her eyes with a lace hankie somewhere in the background, Aunt Dorothy spilling champagne on someone's good dress. Both the aunts, who'd always been there for me since I was born, loving me with no conditions attached, no conditions whatsoever.

I went down the steps of the terrace, trying not to listen to the sad little doves calling all around the garden. It seemed a pity that such a perfect garden wouldn't be the setting now for a wedding. Piriel and Dad didn't know what they were missing. All that work the aunts had done, getting everything so beautiful – it would be hard having to be the one to break the news to them. Perhaps I should start with Aunt Dorothy first, then we could tell Aunty Nat together. It might be easier that way. Aunt Dosh was always so peaceful, things never seemed as bad when she was around. She most definitely *wasn't* a loser; Dad was wrong about that.

The watering can wasn't in the summerhouse, nor was Aunt Dorothy. She wasn't anywhere in the back garden. I hesitated, then set off down the path that led to the creek, through the bush block that Piriel said Aunty Nat should sell. Piriel, I thought, had far too *many* opinions about what the aunts should or shouldn't do! It wasn't really any of her business, what they did with Avian Cottage or the land around it. Anyone would think she was the ice-lady, the way she tried to manipulate people, bend them to her will so that they caused the least amount of inconvenience to her own life . . .

I could hear the creek gurgling away to itself further down. It was really stupid, the way I hadn't bothered to explore this part of the garden yet. Aunt Dosh was always telling me how pretty it was, that I needn't be so scared of snakes, because she hadn't seen any at all. It *was* pretty, too. I could help rake up the dry stuff and burn it off, I thought. If Corrie Ryder and I *both* got stuck into it, we'd clear it all away in no time. You wouldn't need to feel nervous about snakes if Corrie was around; she wasn't scared of *anything*. In fact, if you were marooned on a desert island, Corrie would be excellent company.

Aunt Dosh was down by the creek. I could see the crown of her old straw hat with the red band tied around it. Dad, I remembered, grinning to myself, had once given her a very expensive pith helmet, because he couldn't stand the sight of that battered old hat she wore in summer. Aunt Dosh hadn't liked the new helmet. It was on the floor of her wardrobe, holding all the socks she meant to darn some time or other. I jumped down the last bit of steep path, then stopped, not going any further. I stayed right where I was, peering through the bushes. Aunt Dorothy was sitting under a tree, but she wasn't by herself. Ed Woodley was next to her. There was a heart carved in the bark of the tree, with initials inside it. They both looked very happy sitting under their initials, holding hands . . .

12

. . . .

Some things that aren't *too* bad about Parchment Hills

1. Everyone talks to you.

2. Birds singing all over the place.

3. Watching the stars before going to sleep.

4. All the houses are so old they're probably still going to be here in fifty years' time, not looking much different except for new coats of paint.

5. Having someone living right next-door who might be able to work out *Rulers of Cedrona.*

6. Having a friend my own age living right next-door.

7. Horace likes it here. He has favourite places in the garden.

8. *I* like it here. *I've* got favourite places in the garden.

Some things that aren't *too* bad about Corrie Ryder

1. Horace likes her heaps.

2. She doesn't make you feel dumb when you can't do things. She just shows you how.

3. She's got a nice kookaburra laugh.

4. What you see is what you get.

5. She can be really funny and cheers you up when you feel down.

6. If you went to the same school as her, she'd never be nice to you one minute and nasty the next. If she ever got mad at you she'd come right out and tell you why. Then things would be okay again.

7. If you were really poor and didn't have any shoes, she'd probably take hers off and *give* them to you. (Not that beggars or anyone would want to wear Corrie Ryder's shoes!)

8. I wouldn't mind going to the same school as Corrie. I wouldn't mind being her friend, either. I'd feel kind of lucky . . .

NB I'm getting a bit fed up with lists! Maybe I won't write so many from now on.

. . . .

It wasn't a good time to grab Aunty Nat's attention, not when she was stocking the fridge. She always treated that job like some fascinating hobby. I passed her the next supermarket bag, trying to think of good opening sentences. The two problems were crashing around inside my head. They felt as distracting as separate tapes being played together.

1. I rang Dad while you were out shopping.

2. There's something going on right under your nose, and I think you should know about it. Ed Woodley's got a crush on . . .

3. By the way, there's been a slight change of plans about Dad's wedding.

4. Sit down, Aunty Nat, and I'll make you a cup of tea.

It was hard to compete with celery being trimmed and stacked cut-side down in a pink plastic dish, freezer use-by dates getting checked as carefully as visas, and a hiding place being found for this week's supply of fruit yoghurt (so Aunt Dorothy couldn't eat it all in one go). I passed her another supermarket bag.

1. I know you don't like travelling anywhere by plane, but . . .

2. This might come as a shock, but do you realise a certain person has a crush on Aunt Dosh and she has one right back?

3. Dad and Piriel decided that . . .

4. Sit down, Aunty Nat, and I'll make you a nice cup of tea.

'There, that's the perishables out of the way,' she said. 'Now for the rest of the stuff. Careful with that jar of stuffed olives; it's part of the wedding menu.'

'Aunty Nat,' I began in a throttled voice that didn't sound like my own. 'I rang Dad while you were out shopping . . .'

'Oh goody, you managed to get on to him, then? Sometimes he's a bit hard to track down at the Sydney office. That snooty receptionist always sounds like it's beneath her dignity to put calls through . . . What do you think about these fancy serviettes? Maybe plain white would have been better, but then I noticed these ones with the cute little silver horseshoes.'

She'd also bought two special champagne glasses, with 'bride' stencilled on one, and 'groom' on the other. They had bows of ribbon tied to the stems and were really hideous, but she put them tenderly away on a shelf as though they were Oscar awards. I *couldn't* tell her! And it wasn't *fair*, I thought despairingly, that Dad had even asked me to! It was just as unfair, really, as Tara McCabe scratching the duco on Mrs H.'s car at school, then bribing a dim little Year Five kid into taking the blame. (The bribe was the promise of a pony ride if that kid ever happened to be passing through Gippsland!)

'Sarah, instead of standing there having a good old gnaw at that fingernail, try to come up with some groovy ideas for lunch. I thought I'd make something special, seeing it's Ed's last day.'

'Sit down, Aunty Nat, and I'll make you a nice cup of tea,' I said, then blabbed, 'Do you realise he's got a crush on Aunt Dorothy and she's got one right back?'

'Thanks, but it's a bit too near lunchtime for a cuppa. And yes, I *do* know about Ed and Dosh, as a matter of fact,' Aunty Nat said calmly. 'I wouldn't call it just a *crush*, though. Not when they've made plans to buy that creek block from me and build a cottage down there. Mind you, Dosh was going to tell you herself pretty soon, so make sure you act surprised when she does. For some reason she's always accusing me of being a bit of a chatterbox.'

'You mean . . . they're getting *married?*'

'Well, I certainly *hope* that's what they have in mind, dear. Ed's buying her an engagement ring soon, and Dosh mentioned an autumn wedding, because the trees in the garden will look so handsome then. It's wonderful for them both. And for me, too, that I'll have them living so close. I really thought you might have guessed what was in the air already, with her being more daffy than usual and actually managing to quit smoking, too. We'll have a party when they announce it officially. Inviting all the card people, of course, and everyone we know up here in Parchment Hills. Let's hope Dosh doesn't lose her new ring beforehand, though, grubbing about in the garden. My word, *two* weddings at Avian Cottage in the one year . . .'

Like a coward, I retreated downstairs, stopping on the landing to pat the carved eagle. It was a habit I'd got into, having grown quite fond of that eagle. It seemed to add a touch of character to the house. Ed Woodley had installed a brass coach-lamp underneath, which also added a touch of character. He hadn't charged Aunty Nat for the lamp, saying it was a house-warming gift. He was nice, really, always being so patient when Aunty Nat had changed her mind a hundred times about wallpaper and colour schemes, rushing down to the terrace to make sure Aunt Dorothy hadn't hurt herself when she fell off the retaining wall, climbing up the willow tree to rescue Horace when he got stuck, calling me 'Sally'. It was good news about him and Aunt Dorothy. Later on, I thought, I'd go and tell them so, but there was the other thing to be dealt with first. It *had* to be got out of the way. Something happy shouldn't be jumbled up with something else that felt . . . unhappy.

Aunty Nat would have to be told straight after lunch, I decided, knowing it couldn't be postponed much longer than that. On top of everything else, she'd need time to get used to the idea of an unexpected interstate trip. Both the aunts would. (Unlike Dad and Piriel, they didn't have much practice in dashing off to places at short notice.) Even that New Zealand holiday had been a huge event in their lives. They'd spent weeks planning what to take, trying to fit it all in the suitcases, then dumping everything out and starting again. Because of having plenty of suitcase experience from boarding school, I'd packed for them both in the end. It wouldn't be necessary for this trip, though, as we'd just be flying there and back in the one day. That was going to be difficult enough, with the aunts so nervous about planes. Another difficult thing was the ghastly dress Aunty Nat had ordered at a Parchment Hills shop for the wedding. She'd fallen in love with it. Her size hadn't been in stock, and they'd promised to get one in by Friday next week. But Friday next week would be too late . . .

And what was *I* going to wear? Although the wedding had been pared down to something that would probably last just a few minutes, and even if we'd be the only guests now (and by the sound of it, not *really* expected to be there), it still seemed wrong to show up for it in everyday clothes. As though it was nothing more important than some kind of business meeting.

I went along the passage and checked my wardrobe, finding nothing suitable. If Piriel hadn't had time to make up that dress, I thought moodily, then she should have passed the job on to Aunty Nat. It would have just been a matter of posting the material and pattern out to Avian Cottage. (Except Piriel never seemed to use ordinary mail; it was always couriers and fax messages.) Aunty Nat would have found time, somehow, to sew it up. She *always* managed to find time, for anything needed, for whatever was asked of her. I closed the wardrobe door, feeling depressed, then remembered the money Dad had given me for holiday outings. In spite of the list I'd made of places to visit and things to do, most of that money still hadn't been touched. (The things on my list hadn't been done, either, but that was another matter.) Without telling Aunty Nat, I sneaked out and headed for the shops, not feeling particularly hopeful even when I got there.

Parchment Hills had only two clothing shops, and the first had nothing at all in my size. The other, more showy one, was where Aunty Nat had ordered her outfit for the wedding. In fact, it seemed to *specialise* in clothes that people like Aunty Nat would buy for a wedding, I thought, sleuthing through racks of dresses that all seemed to tie at the neckline with a large

208

floppy bow. The assistant tried to be helpful, though the details I gave her were useless. I didn't even know *myself* what I was searching for.

'You'd be better off trying the little place across the street, Sarah,' she said. 'That always has clothes for young people.'

'I didn't know there was another . . .' I began, then realised she'd called me by my name, probably remembering it from when I'd been there with Aunty Nat.

Stupidly, the fact that she had remembered my name brought a lump to my throat. It stayed there while I followed directions and crossed the street, to a little shop I'd never even noticed before, near the railway station.

The girl behind the counter looked even more dreamy than Aunt Dorothy. She glanced up from a magazine, smiled vaguely, then went on reading as though maybe it was *my* shop and I could do whatever I liked in it. I didn't really mind that there wasn't someone saying, 'May I help you, madam?' as they did at the Moreton Centre. It wasn't likely that I'd be in there for very long, because most of the stuff looked like rubbish. It wasn't arranged in any particular order of junk, either. Everything was just bundled together, handbags and sequinned shoes jostling each other for floor space, scarves fluttering from the ceiling, assorted clothing slung any old way on a big creaky circular rack. There were even winter clothes mixed up with all the summery things.

I took down a skirt, looked at it, but shoved it right back. (No one in their right mind would wear what seemed to be three different coloured umbrellas sewn together.) Then came baggy patchwork trousers, a dress with a hemline cut into castle turret shapes, a jacket striped like a canvas deckchair, purple leggings with ladybirds all over them, and a waistcoat fastened with little mirrors instead of buttons. I began to feel less down in the dumps. The clothes might be junk, but they were all so *merry*. You couldn't, for instance, drape yourself in an enormous sentry-red scarf fringed with gold coins and still feel glum. The girl behind the counter yawned lazily and turned the pages of her magazine. I put the scarf back and spun the rack, scooping through bright satin shirts, a yellow polka-dot raincoat, something that looked as though it belonged on a skating rink, something with feathers, a velvet dress . . .

It was green, almost the same colour as the plants Corrie Ryder had given me. Like everything else in the shop, it didn't really make any attempt to be serious. The sleeves were tight to the elbows, then opened out like bells, lined with material printed in an acorn pattern. There were more acorns, little bronze ones, jingling around the neckline. Those acorns would probably come off and get lost, I thought automatically. Velvet couldn't be washed, so you'd have to keep sending it to the drycleaners. It was an impractical dress, and the person who'd designed it obviously didn't follow Piriel's rules about classic styles that could be mixed and matched. Whoever bought it would have to be *crazy*. But even while I was lecturing myself about all that, I found I'd somehow stepped behind the changing-room curtain to try it on.

On the way back up the hill to Avian Cottage, I kept stopping to peer into the dress-shop bag. If I wore that dress in Sydney, where they were having even hotter summer weather, I'd probably *melt*. Piriel would no doubt think it was a stupid choice, and she'd be right. There wouldn't be any way of explaining that I'd bought it because all the other clothes I'd ever owned made me blend into the background, but this one seemed to snatch me right out of it. Also, that I just simply *liked* it.

The hill didn't seem quite so steep today. Usually, after running messages for the aunts, I'd stomp up that long slope wondering crossly why they couldn't have found somewhere flatter to live. It wasn't too bad, though, if you took your time. The dog behind the wire fence at Number Eleven didn't yip hysterically as it normally did, perhaps because I was just ambling by in no hurry. It just barked once, then shut up, as though I'd been recognised now as a legitimate resident in the street. (Next time, I thought, I might even get a tail-wag.) Past the red cedar cottage where a bad-tempered old man lived (though he *had* helped us restart the car once when it conked out on the slope); past the Country Women's Association president's house (Aunty Nat had already joined and was well on the way to getting herself put on their committee), and the young couple's place (they were expecting a baby in May; Aunty Nat had already ordered one of Eileen Holloway's *Peter Pan and Wendy* mugs for the poor little thing).

I stopped and glanced back down at Parchment Hills shopping centre. There wasn't very much of it. From the top of the hill it resembled a finger painting; you almost expected the sun to have a cosy face drawn on it. Even the train at the railway station looked as though it might puff out a balloon of poster-colour smoke at any moment. On the far side of the station was a belt of trees, a sports oval, then the district secondary college, where Corrie Ryder went. To get there, you didn't even have to go down the hill and through the shopping centre. There was a short cut over the other side of the creek. Corrie had told me about it. She always picked up a friend of hers on the way, and they walked together, then came home together when school finished. It must be nice, I thought, to be able to do something like that day after day.

When I reached Avian Cottage, Aunty Nat was on the porch, fussing about with the ornamental urns Mr Ryder had lent her. Last week she'd filled them with white pot-plant flowers – getting ready for the wedding. My feet seemed to stall. She'd have to be told that those flowers wouldn't be needed, and I should do it right *now*.

'Oh, there you are, Sarah,' Aunty Nat called over her shoulder, and I went slowly down to the porch and saw that she was actually *removing* the white plants, then stacking the empty urns into a carton. 'You might have mentioned you were nicking off somewhere, dear. I thought we had all that out when you took off into town the other day without letting us know first.'

'Sorry,' I said. 'Aunty Nat, there's something . . .'

'It's just as well the postie was running late today and saw you down at the shops, otherwise I might have been worried. We've had lunch, but yours is keeping warm in the oven. Soon as you've finished eating, you could take these urns back next-door. We won't be needing them now they've picked Sydney instead.'

I craned around one of the barley-sugar porch posts, trying to catch a glimpse of her face, to see how upset she was. It was hard to guess from her back view, which was just a busy whirr of plastic gloves wiping out the urns, and refugee plants being given a new home in the flowerbed next to the steps.

'You already *know*?' I faltered. '*I* was supposed to tell you about that. Dad asked me to, when I rang him this morning. But I just didn't know *how* to . . .'

Aunty Nat got up from her knees and peeled off the gloves, flapping them about to get rid of loose dirt. When she turned around, I saw with relief that she didn't look upset at all. She was *annoyed*, which was much easier to cope with.

'As far as I'm concerned, it wasn't even *your* job to tell me!' she snapped. 'I'm cranky as a snake with your dad for being so offhand about the whole thing. *And*

213

having the cheek to start blustering when he found out you hadn't passed on the message yet! Oh well, at least it means I can clear these urn thingummybobs out of the way. It was a pain trying to fit the key in the lock and not knock any of them over.'

'Is he really mad with me? I *should* have told you. It's all my fault . . .'

'Nonsense! Piriel could have easily let us know, anyway, before she left. I'm cheesed off with *both* of them, and I don't mind saying so. That phone was just about blistering by the time I finished with your dad, I can tell you!'

'Did he ring here again?'

'No, I was the one who put the call through, though it was just by chance. Lunchtime, while you were off gallivanting. All of a sudden I realised we didn't have a clue what to order in the way of drinks for the wedding, so I thought I'd better ring Brett and check. You know what a big song and dance he always makes about wine. So *that's* how I found out, and I can't help feeling as though I deserved a bit more consideration from him and Piriel. Never mind, lovie, there's no need for you to look frazzled. It's certainly not *you* I'm cross with. Except don't ever nick off anywhere again without telling me first, madam, particularly not round about meal times! The very idea . . .'

'I'm sorry . . . about Sydney,' I said miserably.

Aunty Nat left off scolding and peered at me.

'You made them a cake. And it's not going to be any

214

use taking it up to them. I don't mean because it might get squashed, either. They won't even be around to *eat* it, they're just leaving straight after . . . straight after the registry office . . .'

Aunty Nat shooed me in through the front door with her rubber gloves.

'Your beautiful cake! And the summerhouse, all painted and ready for –'

'Doesn't matter,' she said evenly. 'That summer-house is for *us*, anyhow, when all's said and done. We wanted it looking nice. Besides, Dosh might want to use it for *her* wedding, though I bet you anything she'll trip on the steps or do something else just as daft. Come and eat your lunch, and I'll have a cup of tea, to keep you company.'

I stared blurrily down at the plate she set on the kitchen table. It held two baked potatoes stuffed with salmon in cheese sauce, and there was a salad to go with it. Aunty Nat had made me a special one, a kind of joke between us which dated back to preschool days. To coax me to eat salad then, she'd make a little person from a pear half, with punk carrot hair, lettuce-leaf skirt, and shoes cut from tomato quarters. Looking at it now somehow made me want to blub. I ate a celery sock and the beetroot handbag, then had to stop rather quickly and fumble for the tissues which were kept on the bench. The tissue-box cover, I noticed, was new. Aunty Nat had made it from scraps of the cloud curtain material. She'd stitched a double lace frill around the opening, and embroidered a little blue bird on one side. It wasn't, I thought tearfully, the sort of object you'd find in Piriel's kitchen. Half a dozen tissues later, I blew my nose and said, 'They don't even *want* us there, you know.'

'Well, I think we should give them the benefit of the doubt and show up for it,' Aunty Nat said. 'Can I have my damp shoulder back now, dear, if you've finished with it? We won't travel up by plane, though, thanks very much. That passenger in the film did a pretty nifty job landing a big jet, but I wouldn't fancy having to rely on Dosho. We'll go by rail. I'll ring up later and get his secretary to book train seats and maybe a hotel reservation if we decide to stay overnight. I could easily manage all that myself, of course, but it will give her something to do instead of sitting there buffing away at her nails.'

'They only want each other, nobody else,' I said, still aboard the train of my own thoughts. 'I don't mean just the wedding, either . . . it's how things *are*. They'd honestly rather have that apartment all to themselves, too. I'd only be in their way if I moved in. It's just that they don't know how to come right out and say it.'

Aunty Nat refilled her cup, stirring in sugar with a little spoon she'd bought. It had a kookaburra on the top.

Her birthday and Christmas presents were going to be a cinch from now on, I thought absently. It would just be a matter of searching around for bird motif teaspoons, so she could end up with a whole appalling collection. The junkshops in Parchment Hills would always be a good place to look.

'If I lived at Avian Cottage all the time . . .' I said.

'Is that what you'd like to do, dear?'

'Yes. That's what I'd like to do. Maybe I've got a nerve suggesting it, though. It's putting you on the spot.'

'Rubbish! I've *never* gone along with that boarding-school idea, not when you could have had a perfectly good home with us all these years. I'd *love* to have you here. So would Dosh.'

She was beaming, I noticed, as though she might clap her hands at any minute.

'If I lived here, I could go to the same school as Corrie Ryder,' I said. 'She knows this short cut over the other side of the creek.'

'As long as you don't both go larking around and getting your good school shoes wet.'

'I could still go in to visit whenever they asked me. Piriel was going to buy a fold-out couch for the spare room at the apartment. I can sleep on that when I visit them both. It should work out okay, don't you think?'

'I don't see why not,' Aunty Nat said. 'Maybe when you start that acting course, you could stay overnight at the same time. Saturdays, wasn't it? Mind you, I've got more than a faint suspicion you're not exactly over the moon about that workshop business.'

'Well, I don't see how I'll be able to fit it in, really.

217

Not *every* Saturday. If I'm living out here, I'll want to be doing other things with Corrie on the weekends.'

'Fair enough, but you'd better let them know pretty soon. Then the place can go to someone else and Piriel will get a refund. Goodness, all these things to arrange, so many loose ends to tie up . . .'

'It's all right, Aunty Nat. You won't have to do any fighting this time. *I'll* ask him. About changing schools and living here with you and everything.'

'Well, I'll be standing right there beside you when you tackle the asking,' Aunty Nat said. 'Backing you up, and so will Dorothy. There are certain things that can't and shouldn't be sorted out over the phone, though, Sarah. When we're in Sydney might be the best time. Maybe you'd better make a list of what you want to actually say . . .'

'I'm sick to death of lists,' I said. 'I don't need one this time, anyhow. When we get there, I probably won't have too much trouble working out what to say.'

'We'll have to pack an overnight bag each for Sydney. And talking clothes, I notice you've got a dress-shop bag there . . . Did you buy something new while you were down the street?'

'Just a minute while I shake it out properly, so you can see how it looks.'

'Oh, it's *lovely*, Sarah!' Aunty Nat said. 'But isn't it a funny time of the year to get yourself a winter dress? They don't usually have them in stock quite this early, either. It's *beautiful*, even if it *is* a bit dizzy. Still, everyone your age should have a dizzy kind of dress once in a while. Did you have Sydney in mind when you bought it, dear? Might be a bit hot, you know, though I daresay there'll be air-conditioning at that registry office . . .'

'I don't think I'll take it up to Sydney,' I said. 'That's not what I bought it for, really. It's kind of special, to wear at Aunt Dorothy's wedding. But right now, I'll just nip over next-door and show Corrie.'

ABOUT THE AUTHOR

Born in Kempsey, New South Wales, Robin Klein has now had more than forty books published. Many have been shortlisted for the Australian Children's Book of the Year Award, including *People Might Hear You* (1984), *Hating Alison Ashley* (1985), *Halfway Across the Galaxy and Turn Left* (1986) and *Seeing Things* (1994).

Came Back to Show You I Could Fly won a Human Rights Award for Literature in 1989. It also won the 1990 Australian Children's Book of the Year Award for older readers, and was shortlisted for the 1990 Victorian Premier's Literary Award and the 1990 NSW Premier's Literary Award. This outstanding novel was named a White Raven book at the 1990 Bologna Children's Book Fair.

More recently, Robin's stories about the Melling sisters have been highly acclaimed: *All in the Blue Unclouded Weather*, which was followed by *Dresses of Red and Gold* and *The Sky in Silver Lace*, was winner of the 1992 NSW Premier's Award for Literature (Children's Books).

In 1991 Robin Klein was awarded the Dromkeen Medal for her significant contribution to the appreciation and development of children's literature in Australia. She lives with one of her four children in the hills near Melbourne, where she writes full-time.

MORE GREAT READING FROM PUFFIN

☆☆☆☆☆☆☆☆☆☆☆☆☆☆☆☆☆☆☆☆☆☆☆☆☆☆☆☆

All in the Blue Unclouded Weather   Robin Klein

One summer in the late 1940s, in the blue unclouded weather of the post-war years, the Melling girls are growing up. These are sisters you'll never forget.

Winner of the Children's Book Award in the 1992 NSW Premier's Literary Awards. A Children's Book Council of Australia Notable Book, 1992.

Dresses of Red and Gold   Robin Klein

It's autumn in the tiny Australian town of Wilgawa and the Melling girls are preparing for a wedding. But autumn also brings uncertainty for the Mellings – their carefree world may never be the same.

The Sky in Silver Lace   Robin Klein

The delightful Melling sisters are back in this third collection of interlinked short stories about their friendships and dreams, their hopes and joys. Funny and thoughtful, this book lingers long in the memory.

Came Back to Show You I Could Fly   Robin Klein

The moving and powerful story of eleven-year-old Seymour's friendship with the beautiful eighteen-year-old Angie. Beneath Angie's glitter lies the tragedy which is the world of drugs.

Winner of the 1990 CBC Book of the Year Award for Older Readers. Winner of the 1989 Australian Human Rights Award. Shortlisted for the 1990 NSW and Victorian Premiers' Literary Awards.
Now a feature film (Say a Little Prayer).
Winner of the 1992 Canberra's Own Outstanding List Award (COOL) Secondary Division.

MORE GREAT READING FROM PUFFIN

☆☆☆☆☆☆☆☆☆☆☆☆☆☆☆☆☆☆☆☆☆☆☆☆☆☆☆☆☆☆

The Lake at the End of the World   Caroline Macdonald

It is 2025 and the world has been cleared of all life by a chemical disaster. But then Diana meets Hector ...

Winner of the 1989 Alan Marshall Award, named an Honour Book in the 1989 CBC Book of the Year Awards and shortlisted for the NSW Premier's Award. Runner-up for the 1990 Guardian Children's Fiction Award.

Looking for Alibrandi   Melina Marchetta

Josephine Alibrandi feels she has a lot to bear – the poor scholarship kid in a wealthy Catholic school, torn between two cultures, and born out of wedlock. This is her final year of school, the year of emancipation. A superb book.

Winner of the 1993 CBC Book of the Year Award for Older Readers.
Winner of the 1993 Kids' Own Australian Literary Award (KOALA).
Winner of the 1993 Variety Club Young People's Talking Book of the Year Award.
Winner of the 1993 Australian Multicultural Children's Literature Award.

The House Guest   Eleanor Nilsson

The HBS is getting better and better at its dangerous games. Gunno, Jess, Wally and Pete make a great team – until the fateful day when they discover the old secluded house in the valley. After that, nothing is the same again ...

Winner of the 1992 CBC Book of the Year Award for Older Readers.
Winner of the 1992 SA Festival Award for Literature (Children's Books).
Winner of the 1992 Victorian Premier's Literary Award (Children's Books).